I0671781

Shark Santoyo Crime Series

BY

BETHANY MAINES

Blue Zephyr Press
2661 N. Pearl, #360
Tacoma WA 98407

This book is a work of fiction. Names, characters, and incidents are products of the author's imagination or are used fictiously. Any resemblance to actual events or persons living or dead is entirely coincidental.

Copyright © 2018, 2025 by Bethany Maines

All rights reserved, including the right to reproduce this book or portions thereof in any form whatsoever.

Cover art by **LILTdesign.com**.

ISBN-10: 1-7320863-3-8
ISBN-13: 978-1-7320863-3-3

DEDICATION

Dedicated, with many thanks, to:

Sue Owen

TABLE OF CONTENTS

CONTENTS

SHARK'S BITE

PROLOGUE
Six Months Ago

Peregrine: Durrville

Seventeen-year-old Peregrine Hays stood at the entrance of the construction yard with her hands on her knees, panting and squinting through a light summer rain. Below her, a giant spool of electrical cable bounced down the slope toward the road at the base of the hill, picking up speed as flames—fed by the gasoline she'd doused it in—ate into the wood and wire.

Timing is everything.

At the bottom of the hill, the road's asphalt pavement, still warm from the heat of the day and illuminated by street lights, steamed as raindrops splattered down. And on the road, three teenage girls, dressed only in lingerie, were stumbling toward a van, pushed and herded at every faltering step by Luciana and Isabella. Three men sprinted after them, their angry shouts indecipherable to Peri. What had started as a good-sized lead was closing quickly as the barefoot teenagers were barely managing to stay upright.

The massive spool spun toward the men, fiery whips of plastic-encased wire spun off like arcs of lightning. If Peri had timed this right, the spool would strike the road just before the men. If she were truly lucky it would run them over.

One man finally looked up and shouted, pointing at the

flaming wheel bearing down on them. They slowed, then began to run back the way they had come.

Peri thought with regret that they were probably going to escape. But that was acceptable because so would her friends. She began to jog back down the hill. Her lungs still burned from her all out sprint up to the construction yard, but she didn't have time for a real recovery.

She had only taken a few steps when two bikers, their jackets emblazoned with the red devil of the Vagos motorcycle club, rounded the corner. Peri felt herself mouth the word "shit," but no sound came out. The Vagos weren't a part of this. No one else was supposed to be involved. The fireball was only supposed to be for the damn sex traffickers. All others need not apply.

The bikers hit their brakes, skidding as their wheels locked up on the wet road. The bikers went down—their rides continuing forward into the hell mouth of the flaming spool. The bikes ignited and then exploded. The motorcyclists struggled to their feet and Peri breathed out a sigh of relief. Not waiting around to see what else could go wrong, she ran down the hill to the van.

"Get in," she yelled to the stragglers.

"Fuck me," gasped Isabella. Her dark, chola-style eyeliner was melting down her face in the rain.

"All of you, get in the van!" repeated Peri, shoving the girls at the open doors.

Luciana was already climbing into the driver's seat as Isabella and Peri pushed the three shivering girls into the back. Luciana hit the gas and the van roared into life, tires squealing against the wet pavement before launching forward. Lurching with the movement, Peri climbed into the passenger seat.

"You know," said Luciana, "when you said you needed to borrow my van, this wasn't quite what I had in mind."

"I told you what we'd be doing. You didn't have to come," said Peri.

Luciana gave her a look. "We could have called the cops."

"The girls would have been gone by the time the police got there. *If* the police got there. I told Isabella I'd get her sister back. You think I should have waited?"

"I think that could have gone really badly," said Luciana.

"We got the girls," said Peri, twisting in her seat to look at them—they all looked varying degrees of high and two of them had visible bruises on their faces and arms. The third looked like she hadn't eaten in weeks. "That's what counts."

Being high was to be expected. Most of the girls who got trafficked were kept on one substance or another. It kept them from trying to escape. Running from the men who were selling them had been a testament to their willpower to survive.

"Sofia?" asked Isabella, grabbing her sister's arm. "Sofia, are you OK?"

Sofia turned away from the back window and the orange flames and focused on Isabella's face as if seeing it for the first time. "No," she said.

"You're going to be," said Isabella, hugging her sister. "I got you back now. You're going to be fine."

Peri exchanged a glance with Luciana. They both knew the stats on girls who had escaped sex slavery. Fine was a relative term.

PROLOGUE
Six Months Ago

Peregrine: Durrville

Seventeen-year-old Peregrine Hays stood at the entrance of the construction yard with her hands on her knees, panting and squinting through a light summer rain. Below her, a giant spool of electrical cable bounced down the slope toward the road at the base of the hill, picking up speed as flames—fed by the gasoline she'd doused it in—ate into the wood and wire.

Timing is everything.

At the bottom of the hill, the road's asphalt pavement, still warm from the heat of the day and illuminated by street lights, steamed as raindrops splattered down. And on the road, three teenage girls, dressed only in lingerie, were stumbling toward a van, pushed and herded at every faltering step by Luciana and Isabella. Three men sprinted after them, their angry shouts indecipherable to Peri. What had started as a good-sized lead was closing quickly as the barefoot teenagers were barely managing to stay upright.

The massive spool spun toward the men, fiery whips of plastic-encased wire spun off like arcs of lightning. If Peri had timed this right, the spool would strike the road just before the men. If she were truly lucky it would run them over.

One man finally looked up and shouted, pointing at the

flaming wheel bearing down on them. They slowed, then began to run back the way they had come.

Peri thought with regret that they were probably going to escape. But that was acceptable because so would her friends. She began to jog back down the hill. Her lungs still burned from her all out sprint up to the construction yard, but she didn't have time for a real recovery.

She had only taken a few steps when two bikers, their jackets emblazoned with the red devil of the Vagos motorcycle club, rounded the corner. Peri felt herself mouth the word "shit," but no sound came out. The Vagos weren't a part of this. No one else was supposed to be involved. The fireball was only supposed to be for the damn sex traffickers. All others need not apply.

The bikers hit their brakes, skidding as their wheels locked up on the wet road. The bikers went down—their rides continuing forward into the hell mouth of the flaming spool. The bikes ignited and then exploded. The motorcyclists struggled to their feet and Peri breathed out a sigh of relief. Not waiting around to see what else could go wrong, she ran down the hill to the van.

"Get in," she yelled to the stragglers.

"Fuck me," gasped Isabella. Her dark, chola-style eyeliner was melting down her face in the rain.

"All of you, get in the van!" repeated Peri, shoving the girls at the open doors.

Luciana was already climbing into the driver's seat as Isabella and Peri pushed the three shivering girls into the back. Luciana hit the gas and the van roared into life, tires squealing against the wet pavement before launching forward. Lurching with the movement, Peri climbed into the passenger seat.

"You know," said Luciana, "when you said you needed to borrow my van, this wasn't quite what I had in mind."

"I told you what we'd be doing. You didn't have to come," said Peri.

Luciana gave her a look. "We could have called the cops."

"The girls would have been gone by the time the police got there. *If* the police got there. I told Isabella I'd get her sister back. You think I should have waited?"

"I think that could have gone really badly," said Luciana.

"We got the girls," said Peri, twisting in her seat to look at them—they all looked varying degrees of high and two of them had visible bruises on their faces and arms. The third looked like she hadn't eaten in weeks. "That's what counts."

Being high was to be expected. Most of the girls who got trafficked were kept on one substance or another. It kept them from trying to escape. Running from the men who were selling them had been a testament to their willpower to survive.

"Sofia?" asked Isabella, grabbing her sister's arm. "Sofia, are you OK?"

Sofia turned away from the back window and the orange flames and focused on Isabella's face as if seeing it for the first time. "No," she said.

"You're going to be," said Isabella, hugging her sister. "I got you back now. You're going to be fine."

Peri exchanged a glance with Luciana. They both knew the stats on girls who had escaped sex slavery. Fine was a relative term.

Thursday ~ December 1

Shark: Rolling Thunder Lanes, Grand Opening

So far no one had threatened to cut anyone's balls off. Shark Santoyo was calling that a win.

It was nine on a Thursday night and he was on his fifth loop of the interior of Rolling Thunder Lanes. He had decided up front that no one active in the gang would interact with the public for more than an hour at a time. That seemed to be working, but he couldn't quite believe he was getting away with this. It felt like a giant con.

It *was* a giant con.

But it was also a fully functional bowling alley. When he'd been forced to take leadership of the territory, he'd accepted that he'd have to do business out of a defunct bowling alley. He'd never considered that he'd actually end up running the place as a legit business. Until now.

At the shoe rental booth, Domingo was briefing his replacement as they prepared to change shifts. Domingo had dressed for work in his best gold fronts and sagged jeans. Shark made a mental note to have a conversation with the sixteen-year-old about appropriate work attire. With most of the kids it would be a waste of time, but Domingo was smarter.

Shark could see himself in the mirrored wall of the claw machine by the door. His pale gray eyes stood out against his always tanned skin. His button-down and slacks looked a little too polished for the bowling alley setting, and his prison buzz cut was beginning to grow out. He couldn't decide if more hair made him look older or younger than his barely twenty-six years. He rolled up his sleeves. The hair would have to wait for further consideration.

"Holy shit," said Domingo, finishing up and coming over. "Did you see Peri?"

Shark kept his face expressionless and gave a minor shake of his head, forcing himself not to turn his head like an owl looking for her.

He had last seen Peregrine Hays, the teenage fixer with a fast mouth and even faster knife, two months ago. She'd left his apartment to go comfort her boyfriend over the loss of his mother to cancer and his uncle to a drive-by shooting. Never mind that Peri had gone out of her way to arrange that drive-by.

Never mind that moments before her arms had been wrapped around Shark. She'd left and he'd convinced himself that it was for the best because he was not that kind of guy. Jail-bait was not his thing. It had taken a while, but his brain had kept repeating that until the rest of him got the message. He didn't know why it hadn't occurred to him that she might come to the bowling alley as an actual customer.

Domingo was shaking his head in disbelieving admiration.

"She brought the whole drill team or whatever. And daaaaamn." He pointed to where a group of girls were ordering drinks at the counter. It took Shark a moment to realize that the brunette he was appreciating was Peri.

Peri usually dressed for anonymity, but for once, she looked like the dime piece she was. It took him another moment to realize that Domingo was still talking.

"It freaked me the fuck out. I can't figure out why she doesn't dress like that all the time. Because I mean, she is so totally doable."

Shark quelled the urge to punch him in the face. "Probably because it attracts too much unwanted attention," he said.

"Huh." Domingo looked like he was having an entirely new thought.

Shark walked away, trying to figure out what to say to Peri. He couldn't just leave it. If nothing else, it was going to be a problem if he ever needed to work with her again. By the time he reached her, she was alone in lane four putting on her bowling shoes. He realized that from this angle he could see down her shirt. He had a moment of panic when he realized, as he was contemplating the lacy edge of her bra, that she had noticed him. He dropped down to his elbows on the railing, so he could at least be closer to her face.

When she looked up at him, he realized that he still didn't know what to say. He noticed for the first time that her hazel eyes were made up of little striations of green and gold.

"Can we just stipulate that this is weird and I didn't want to be here anyway and I was forced to come by the drill team? And then maybe skip to the end where we can talk again?"

Shark breathed out a sigh of relief. "If we can stipulate that I didn't want to do this either. And also, what's a drill team?"

"Like generic cheerleaders? I think? I don't know. All I know is that if I hang with them for the rest of the school year I don't have to take PE. Mom's super stoked, she always wanted me to…." She paused as if looking for the right words to encompass her mother's ambitions.

"Have an eating disorder?" suggested Shark, and she grinned. Once again, he was shocked at the clear incompetence of Peri's family. He had always assumed that kids who had mothers that weren't crack whores lived happy well-adjusted lives. Or at the very least didn't carry weaponry and had parents who knew where they were at three in the morning. Peri was showing him otherwise. Where the fuck was her dad? How was her mom so oblivious?

"Why *are* you doing this?" she asked, gesturing to the packed bowling alley.

"My new parole officer doesn't take bribes," he lied. "Suddenly I needed a job, so I figured, how hard could it be? Short answer, by the way, is: harder than you'd think."

"Well, I think most small businesses don't try to staff with gang members."

"I work with what I've got," said Shark.

She looked around. "Turn-out seems good. Leafleting the high school was a good idea."

The bowling alley was pretty packed, actually. He felt a little flare of pride. "Yeah, I think we can make it work for a while."

"Or at least until you can figure out what to do with your PO?" Peri suggested, leaning up against the railing next to him.

"Something like that," he agreed. She really was so much easier to talk to than ninety percent of the people he dealt with.

"Do you think—" Peri began, but stopped as the front door opened and they both turned to look at the new arrivals. It was a habit born out of self-defense, and it amused Shark that she looked at the same time he did.

Vivian Flood strode in, standing literally above the crowd, her face telegraphing disapproval. "And speak of the devil," Shark said sourly.

"Holy shit." Peri scanned Vivian from her white blonde ponytail and glasses, to her miles of leg that ended in a pair of royal blue stacked stilettos. "That's your PO?"

He nodded and hoped Peri bought it. He'd already told Vivian that those shoes were a giveaway. What PO would wear those on the job?

"Seriously? Your parole officer is the Valkyrie's naughty librarian?"

Shark choked on a surprised laugh. "Thanks a lot. Now I'm going to be thinking that every time I see her."

"What do you mean *now*? You weren't thinking that before? She's like one breast plate and a set of horns away from singing opera. Did she park her horse out front?"

Shark crumpled against the railing, trying to hide his laughter. "I'm begging you, please stop."

"Only because you're begging. Believe me, I could go on. I've got a whole riff about Maude Lebowski ready to go. Meanwhile, who's that guy with her?"

A tallish man in a bad suit trailed behind Vivian. "That looks suspiciously like an FBI agent." Shark could not believe what he was seeing. Vivian was reaching new levels of stupidity.

"Really?" Peri stood on her tiptoes to look. "I've never seen one before. Do they all look like such douchebags?"

Shark wanted to smile at her, but he was afraid to with Vivian in the room. "Yes."

"You want me to get rid of him?"

"No, you little serial killer!"

"I didn't say I was going to kill him. There are other ways of getting people out of a building. What's wrong with you?" Her outrage was obviously fake, which was adorable. He'd forgotten how funny she was.

"Just go bowl," he said, because everything else was a conversation he didn't have time for.

"Suit yourself," she said, with a flip of her hair. "Good luck!"

Shark made his way to the bar to meet Vivian. The male agent stalked past them, ignoring Shark. Shark stared after him, trying to figure out why both he and Peri had pegged him as a douchebag immediately. The reaction was instinctual, but what was triggering it?

The agent was about Shark's height and two decades older, with brown hair that Shark thought was touched up at the temples. His suit looked rumpled, like he either didn't own an iron or had been spending too much time sitting in a car. The entire effect was one of uneducated conceit. He was vain without being smart enough to actually have something to be vain about.

"Who the fuck is that guy?" asked Shark quietly, stretching his face into a smile. "And what are you doing here?"

"*That* is ATF Agent Larry Fowler," said Vivian. "And I'm here because he's been burning up my phone asking me what I'm doing about you. So why don't you tell me what you've been doing to piss off the ATF?"

"I have no idea." Shark moved behind the bar. "You're the law and order side of this equation—can't you just ask?"

"No, I can't just ask. They would want to know why I was asking. There would be forms. My boss would have to ask his boss. That's a lot of paper trail. Do you really want that?"

Shark poured himself a drink out of force of habit and to cover his lack of response. No, he didn't want that. He knew how many snitches Geier and The Organization had in the Bureau.

"Meanwhile, what the fuck are you doing?" She waved at the crowd.

"Well," said Shark, "you, my supposed PO, dropped by and told me in front of witnesses that I had to get a legit job or you'd pull my ticket and put me back in prison."

"That was supposed to push Geier into pulling you back into the city!" she snapped.

"And I told you it wouldn't work. Geier doesn't rescue people. I can't make it any clearer. I'm stuck in the suburbs until he wants me back in April. So I had to either come up with a story about how I bribed you or find a legit job. I picked the option I thought you would least object to."

"You are supposed to be helping us get Geier. The FBI didn't pull you out of your cell so you could bowl in the suburbs," she said.

"Keep your fucking voice down," he snarled.

To his surprise, she complied. "I hate the fucking suburbs," she hissed.

"I sympathize," he said, and poured her a shot of vodka.

She downed the shot. "You're going to have to come up with something to deal with Fowler."

Shark was about to reply when he saw Peri coming toward them. He reached for the soda glasses. "That's an interesting perspective, Ms. Flood," he said, as Peri neared.

"Hi!" Peri pitched her voice high, infusing it with that special note of teenage superficiality. "Can I get a cherry Coke?"

Shark filled her glass, not blowing their cover with an outright look of disbelief.

"I'm in lane four. Is there a way we could, like, open a tab?"

Peri pointed at lane four, which had the automatic effect of making both Shark and Vivian follow her gesture to where Larry Fowler the ATF agent was standing, legs spread, arms crossed, in what he probably considered a heroic pose. One of Peri's friends, a brassy blonde, curvaceous and confident, picked up a ball and turned toward Fowler.

"Hey! Perv for brains!" The blonde bellowed the insult, so that she was heard even over the crack of pins and rumble of balls. Most of the room turned to look. "You want to take your hard-on someplace else? We're trying to bowl."

Agent Fowler flushed and stepped back, uncrossing and then re-crossing his arms, trying to regain his composure.

"I'm so sad I don't have that on video," said Shark, forgetting that he was talking to anyone besides Peri.

"That was awesome," agreed Vivian.

"Seriously," called the blonde, "does being a molester make you deaf? Or do I have to call the manager?"

"And that's my cue," said Shark. "Excuse me, ladies."

"Agent Fowler," said Shark, approaching the man who was rapidly leaving the lane four area. "Perhaps we should not stare at the teenagers?"

"You think you can get away with this?" demanded Fowler, poking Shark in the chest. Shark took it, because that was what you did with law enforcement. "You think you can just come in here and change the rules?"

"Agent Fowler, I literally have no idea what you're talking about."

"You should have worked with me. You're going to regret this," said Fowler, and stormed away.

Peri left the bar and winked as she passed Shark, Coke in hand. Goddamn she was hot when she was working. He kept his face neutral, but felt a chill as he saw Vivian watching Peri's walk-away with a thoughtful and attentive expression.

"Whatever his problem is," said Vivian, pulling her eyes away from Peri's retreating figure, "deal with it. We don't have time for this shit."

She walked out and half the room turned to watch her go.

Hours later, when the last patron had finally gone, the doors were locked and Shark had counted the cash into the safe, he finally felt like he could think about his problems. He needed to find Marko—maybe he would have some ideas about Agent Fowler.

His beefy forty-ish bodyguard had, in the last several months, also become his de facto second-in-command. Shark thought, somewhat enviously, that Marko looked like what a gangster ought to look like—olive skin, dark hair, black leather jacket—he could easily fill the role of Bruiser Number Three in any Scorsese film. Marko also ran the crew of leg-breakers known as the Fives who handled debt collection and making book. Third down in rank was the nineteen-year-old and eternally pasty (despite being half-black) Paper, the head of the Blue Street Crew. Blue Street handled merchandise sales—mostly drugs and a few small arms.

When Shark and Marko had arrived a few months ago, the territory had been in disarray, the crews were at each oth-er's throats and their leader, Big Paulie, had been skimming money that he was supposed to be sending to the head of the Organization—Geier.

Shark had taken care of the problem with Big Paulie. Or rather, Big Paulie had taken care of the problem himself, when he'd died of a heart attack two punches into a beatdown from Shark. Not that anyone believed Shark about that. With Peri's help, he'd recovered the cash and returned it to Geier, and the territory was finally running in the black. Personnel issues had been sorted out. Everything was good. Shark had been hoping to simply coast until April, when Geier had promised to call him back into the city. Fowler and Vivian were making that seem less and less likely.

Laughter erupted from the kitchen. He walked in and found the entire crew gathered around Domingo and his phone.

"Have you seen this?" demanded Marko.

"Seen what?"

Domingo cleared his throat. "I... uh... got a text from Peri earlier in the evening. She said to get my phone out and be ready to hit record. So, I did."

He handed Shark his phone. Shark pushed play. The scene with Agent Fowler played out in its entirety. How did Peri think of this shit?

"Can I post it on YouTube?" begged Domingo.

Shark laughed. "Yes, as long as you post it anonymously. Meanwhile, has anyone seen that guy before?"

"I've seen him before," said Paper. "I've loaded his trucks."

"What do you mean?"

"Every few months or so this guy comes through. Big Paulie was the middle man or something. We'd move merchandise from this guy's truck to someone else's truck. Big Paulie would pass out a couple of Benjamins and tell us to keep our mouths shut."

"What kind of merchandise?"

"Dunno. It was in boxes."

"Uh," said Beef. "I saw him last week. He was nosing around, asking about the change of leadership. I gave him the party line—that you and Marko were going to have the territory running clean in no time, that all deals were still in place and no one should worry."

"You didn't tell me about this," snapped Marko, glaring at his long-haired lieutenant.

"We've been fielding questions since Shark took over from Big Paulie. It's been fine! At least, it should have been fine. I don't understand this guy's problem. If he's got some business, he should just come in and renegotiate." Beef adjusted his mandala print t-shirt nervously.

"Maybe," said Shark. "Who knows what kind of shit he was up to with Big Paulie?"

"Oh, for fuck's sake," said Marko. "Big Paulie has been dead for months! How is he still screwing us?"

"I'll take it to Geier in the morning," said Shark. "I'm sure it won't be that big of a deal." Marko eyed him skeptically. In response, Shark subtly rubbed the scar in his eyebrow with his middle finger and Marko hid a laugh behind a handful of fries. Shark agreed with Marko—he was probably lying, but the kids look relieved.

Shark: The Condo

Shark let himself into the corner-unit condo, dropped his keys in the bowl and stared at the depressing collection of personality-free furniture in the living room. Part of being in suburban purgatory was having to live in a condo owned by Geier and The Organization. Not that there was any point in decorating even if he had been paying the rent. And of course he was supposed to be grateful for it. It's a fully furnished condo with two balconies! The furniture was practically cardboard and the kitchen balcony looked over the parking lot. His gratitude could be measured in microns. The only redeeming quality about the place was that it came pre-prepped for weapons storage.

There was a knock on the door and for half a hopeful second he thought it might be Peri. He dismissed the idea almost instantly and opened it to find Vivian standing on the other side. She had let her hair down and removed her glasses. This was closer to her natural state. He suspected that she only wore the glasses as part of her "disguise" of parole officer. He wanted to point out that people made fun of Superman for that shit, but it never seemed like the right time.

"I'll give," she said, "how'd you arrange the teenage bowler? And where can I get one?"

He let her in. "You give me too much credit. I had nothing to do with that. I think he brought that on himself."

"Doesn't matter," she said, walking down the short hallway into the living room, her fingertips trailing along the edge of the bowl that held his keys. "Fowler's blaming you. He's pressuring me to search your place and pull your ticket. He's pissed as hell."

"What are you going to do?" asked Shark. He disliked the way she touched everything in the space.

"I'm searching your place," she said, sitting down on the couch. "Can't you tell?"

"I meant, what are you going to tell him?"

"My established reputation as a straight arrow is coming in handy. I'm going to tell him I couldn't find anything. But I don't think it's going to hold him for long. You'd better come up with something."

"I'd better come up with something? You're FBI. Why aren't you coming up with something?"

"If I give you any help, it could tip our hand. We can't risk exposing you to Geier and losing this whole operation. I'm afraid you're on your own."

"You mean like I have been since I got here? Yeah, thanks for nothing."

Annoyed, Shark went into the kitchen. He'd known that was going to be her answer. He wasn't sure why he was so angry. He'd known he was being used when he agreed to be an informant for the FBI. He'd known he was disposable, he just really hadn't expected it to be rubbed in his face. He'd expected more pretense.

When Vivian had approached him, he had been four years

into a ten-year stint. He had never considered himself the type of person to snitch, but Vivian had offered him something that seemed worthwhile—a new life. With a clean record and a college degree he might actually be able to achieve all the things the teachers had promised would come with education. All he had to do was bring Geier down …and live through it.

He heard Vivian's shoes click on the kitchen tile as she followed him. The sound annoyed him, although it made her easier to track. He ignored her and went to the fridge. Reaching in for a beer, he found Vivian's hand snaking around the front of his pants.

He turned around, furious.

"Come on Shark," she said laughing. "You can't tell me you haven't thought about it. And it's not like you're getting any other perks." When Shark didn't move, she laughed again.

"Just think about it," she smirked, drifting back to the living room. "You might even enjoy it."

If he was really honest with himself, the person he wanted in his bed was Peri, but between her age, her boyfriend and her job, that couldn't happen. Vivian wasn't Peri, but maybe Vivian was right. If she were using him, maybe he ought to be using her.

Angrily, he caught up and spun her around. She responded to his kisses hungrily.

"Take your shoes off," he said, pushing her down on to the couch. "I feel like I'm kissing uphill."

She unbuttoned her jacket. "Make me." Like everything else with Vivian, it seemed that he was in for a fight.

Four Months Ago

Shark & Vivian

Twenty-five year old Shark followed the corrections officer down the hall toward Visiting. He couldn't imagine who would be visiting him. He hoped it wasn't his cellmate's mother again. He didn't know how to console her. He and Chase had both told the fucking CO's that Chase needed to be taken to the shrink. That was supposed to be an automatic transfer to the hospital ward. But nothing had happened. Nothing. And nothing. And nothing. Right up until the morning there had been a fight in the yard between some pumped up Vagos and a Death Head who thought he was tough.

Shark had promised Chase he'd be back in twenty minutes. Twenty minutes had turned into four hours of lockdown, sitting in the hot sun waiting for the bulls to sort everything out between the gangs. Shark didn't give a shit about either one. The rule in prison was stick to your kind and his kind was Latino. That should have put him in with the Vagos, but they were Mexican. And Mexicans hated Puerto Ricans. And despite his gray eyes, there was no way he could mix with the fucking skin-heads. Mostly, he and Chase just tried to keep to themselves, do their time, and keep their backs to a wall. But when he'd finally gotten back to the cell, Chase was dead. He'd hung himself on his sheets. How was Shark supposed to explain to Chase's mother that her son was dead because the CO's don't give two shits about anyone and because a Vagos and a Death Head had decided to settle an old score one morning?

The CO got to the junction in the corridor and turned left instead of right.

"You said I had a visitor," said Shark, hesitating. The officer behind him gave him a shove.

"You do," said the CO. "She's in Interview Eight."

Shark's stare could have bored a hole in the back of the idiot's head. An interview room was not the same as the visiting room. An interview room was for cops. "She who?"

"Don't know. But if she's your lawyer, I want her number."

Shark frowned, trying to figure out what the fuck was going on. The CO pushed him into Interview Eight. He saw the reason for the CO's comment as soon as he crossed the threshold. The blonde sitting on the far side of the table, with her stiletto-clad feet up, was ludicrously hot. If you liked buttoned-down, ice queen types. She was checking her phone.

"You can go," she told the guard.

"He's dangerous. I'll stay to take care of you."

She looked up from her phone. "Fuck off, cocksucker. If I wanted someone to lick my cunt, it wouldn't be a fat fuck who looks like he showers in butter and chicken grease."

"I hope you get raped," said the guard as he slammed the door behind him.

Shark sat down at the table. A speech like that at least deserved some civility. "Hi," he said.

She swung her feet off the table. "Hi." She looked him over and he returned the stare. She was thirty-something, had a rack that other women would pay for, and she was carrying a gun on her hip. She had to be law enforcement, but she didn't feel like law enforcement. "You look like less of an asshole than I thought you would."

"As long as I don't look like I showered in butter and chicken grease."

She laughed. From a bag under the table, she produced a folder, flipped it open, and spread some photos across the table. It was a range of pictures of him with Francesca, probably off her social media. Francesca had always liked to take pictures. The last time he'd seen her was at his sentencing. She'd taken a picture then too.

"Don't worry. I'm sure you'll think of something," she'd said.

Shark had turned to look at her—those blue eyes fixed on him, her black hair settling like a bird's wing next to her face—as she clicked the camera on her phone.

She'd been standing on the audience side of the courtroom wearing Versace. He'd been in handcuffs and a jumpsuit.

"Nothing to say?" asked the tall blonde.

Shark had a lot to say on the topic. He had several hours' worth of a tirade saved up, but he didn't open his mouth. He was a week away from a parole hearing and he couldn't afford any outbursts. He wasn't about to let Francesca win again. He stared mutely at the woman who had apparently dropped out of the atmosphere to torture him.

"You know, I read over your trial transcripts," continued the blonde. "Call me crazy, but I think you got screwed. I think you're in prison for a murder your girlfriend committed. I can't decide if that's incredibly romantic or incredibly stupid."

Four years ago, he'd been halfway through cutting open the safe in the second-story office of Francesca's house when he'd heard Jack de Corvo return home. Jack de Corvo was an art importer with a sprawling house and every free surface decorated with *objets d'arte*. Shark had no problem with the idea of roughing up Jack to steal from him, but it wasn't part of the plan. Jack wasn't supposed to be home for two more hours. Francesca was supposed to be keeping him at a charity event for crippled orphans with one good eye or something. Francesca arrived just after Jack did—they were arguing, yelling as they climbed the stairs. Shark made it out to the landing in time to see Francesca shove her father. In response, Jack had backhanded her against the wall. Shark pushed Jack away and helped Francesca to her feet.

"You little bitch," said Jack, leaning against the balcony railing. "You find some two-bit hood to do your dirty work? You think you're going to steal from me?"

Francesca hadn't replied so much as screamed at him in fury. Then she'd seized a Ming Dynasty vase out of its niche in the wall.

"Don't you dare!" yelled Jack.

Francesca laughed and hurled the vase toward—but not

directly at—her father, aiming to send it crashing to the first floor below. Jack dove for it and reached too far, tumbling over the balcony.

Shark had expected to hear a thump. One story wasn't that high. It should have been a broken leg at worst. But instead of a thump there had been a sickening wet crunch. Francesca and Shark had crept to the edge of the balcony and looked over. Below, Jack de Corvo was impaled on a spiky three-foot-tall bronze sculpture that now protruded through his chest. As they watched, the vase gently rolled out of his hand and dropped onto the floor without a chip.

"We'll bury him in the backyard," said Francesca.

Jack de Corvo made a wheezing noise.

"You'll call an ambulance," Shark said. "You'll tell them there's been an accident."

She wouldn't do it. He'd had to call, and left before the ambulance arrived. But it hadn't mattered. Francesca simply told the police that he'd done it all. In retrospect, perhaps he should have gone with the backyard plan. On the other hand, his voice on the 911 recording had gotten him down to manslaughter instead of murder.

She'd attended every day of the trial, but lied every single time she was called to the stand and at the end of it, all she had to say to him was, "Don't worry. I'm sure you'll think of something."

He'd spent the next four years thinking of crushing comebacks, but now he couldn't remember what he'd actually said. It had probably been, "Go fuck yourself." Which had the benefit of at least being honest, but somewhat lacked in witticism.

"Do you have a point?" Shark asked the blonde, trying not to glance down at her tits.

"My point is, either way—romance or stupidity—if I were you, I'd want out of here," she said. "And if I were you, I'd be looking to maybe expedite the release process."

"I feel like you're winding up for a pitch," said Shark. "Why not just throw the ball?"

She flopped another photo down on the table. It was Geier. Of course, it was Geier. Everything was always about Geier.

Shark rose. "Thanks, but no thanks. You really made my day—telling off Chicken Grease—but I don't snitch."

"But maybe you should." She looked up at him. "You've got a birthday coming up in a couple of months. How many more of those do you want to have in here? And that college degree you got? That makes you a freaking genius in here, but it's not going to do you a fuck's worth of good when you get out in six years and don't have a resume behind it."

"Interesting perspective," said Shark. "But I think I'll run my own life."

He turned to the door.

"You don't," she said. "Run your own life, I mean. But you could. We want to bring Geier down. We could wipe your record. I don't just mean sealed, I mean gone. You could have a nice normal life. And you and upper-crust Barbie here," she tapped the picture of Francesca, "could go do whatever people do when they have fuck tons of Daddy's money to spend."

He glanced back at her. He didn't give two shits about

Francesca. But the idea of being free of Geier… that was tempting. "I've got a parole hearing in a week. I don't need you."

"Maybe I haven't introduced myself," she said. "My name's Vivian Flood. I'm with the FBI and I specialize in ruining people's lives. You're not going to make parole."

Shark felt a spike of adrenaline—the flight or fight response to a threat that he could in no way combat or flee.

"We'll see." He knocked on the door for the guard.

"We will," she agreed. "And I'll be waiting."

Friday ~ December 2

Shark: Kos

Geier cut at his steak with sharp stabs, brutalizing the soft meat with the dull restaurant knife. Shark sat in the booth and drank his water, small sips at a time. Marko stood back a few paces and eyeballed Geier's bodyguard. They all waited for Geier to speak. The restaurant was dedicated to dark wood, snobby waiters and sugar-crusted steaks. Shark wasn't sure of the attraction, but Geier ate one every afternoon and managed his business behind the closed doors while the restaurant staff prepared for dinner service.

From outside came the repetitive ding-ding of a storefront Santa ringing his bell and a cabbie leaning on his horn.

"Third," slice, "time," slice, "this month," said Geier, emphasizing the last words with his knife, which tinged against the china.

Shark was used to Geier's moods, and knew he wasn't to blame for Geier's current pissy one, but the six foot two inch, fifty-ish Geier with the elegant hair had never been narrow-minded when it came to assigning blame. So he kept his mouth shut and held very still. While Geier was in this temper, Shark wasn't even sure he wanted to ask his questions. He needed to get the man into problem-solving mode.

"It's that goddamn Scarecrow Jack mob," said Geier. "Fucking shitheads are stealing my shit."

"The lab guys are certain that it's our product?" Shark kept his tone neutral.

"It's not just the lab guys, it's the street guys." Geier reached in his pocket and pulled out a baggie with white powder in it. "They didn't even bother to re-bag it. They just re-stamped it."

Shark examined the bag. The Organization stamped a red diamond on theirs. Someone had covered the diamond with a black heart, but from the back, the red diamond could still be seen.

"Jacks over fucking diamonds. That's what they're saying on the street. It's not even a fucking congruent simile. It ought to be hearts over diamonds. Or Jacks over The Organization. It's motherfucking asinine uneducated bullshit."

"It's like they never covered grammar in their *How to Sell Drugs* manual," said Shark. Geier's bodyguard shifted in place like a nervous horse.

"Fuck you," growled Geier. "Don't fucking start with me."

"What's the chain of custody?" asked Shark, soothingly. "Where are we losing product?"

"If I knew that, I wouldn't be having this conversation. I would be breaking someone's fucking kneecaps. The only place we've lost a quantity of shit was last year when the Feds hit one of the warehouses. But that shit's in the evidence impound. I even paid some asshat named…" Geier snapped his pale fingers at the bodyguard.

"Fardisburger," supplied the bodyguard, still eyeing Shark with disapproval. Apparently, Geier's bad mood was making everyone nervous.

"I paid Fart Burger to go check on it. He says it's still there. Meanwhile, the Scarecrow is undercutting my prices with my own shit." Geier ground his fork into the thin china until it cracked. Shark watched impassively, turning the problem over in his head.

It didn't sound right. Geier's supply chain, like the rest of The Organization, worked on a system of fear and double-checks. Unless the system had shifted significantly since the last time he was on the outside, it was a fairly difficult proposition to make a significant quantity of product disappear. One or two bags, sure. That was expected. But enough to supply other dealers? That didn't seem likely. He knew where he'd start looking for a leak, if it were him—the one place Geier was sure it wasn't.

"I can look into it for you," he said.

Geier threw the fork down on the table leaving a grease mark on the white table cloth. "Is there no good pussy in the suburbs?" The fingers of his left hand drummed on the table.

"I got that covered," said Shark, eyeing the rise and fall of Geier's long fingers. "You just sound like you could use someone who could get results."

"I'm using Crease."

Shark shrugged and didn't comment. He and Crease had come up about the same time. Crease was resourceful and would probably get it done.

Geier snapped at the bodyguard again. "Seriously, go shove that bell up that Santa's ass. He's killing me." The bodyguard nodded and made for the door, looking relieved to be leaving. Geier re-focused on Shark. "Assuming this isn't just your monthly bid to get back in the city. Why are you here?" A server arrived to swap out the steak and plate for a brand new set.

"An ATF Agent named Larry Fowler has shown up on my doorstep, so to speak. Did Big Paulie ever mention him? Does he have some sort of arrangement with you?"

Geier contemplated his second steak. "No, never heard of him. Why?"

"My guys say he and Big Paulie had a deal of some kind moving merchandise."

"Fucking Big Paulie. Thank God you took care of that guy. What kind of merch?"

"Don't know. It was boxed up. But if it wasn't a sanctioned deal, then…"

"Then what the fuck was it? Well, you'll figure it out. You've always been my problem solver." Geier looked temporarily less annoyed probably because Shark had problems. Someone else having trouble always made Geier feel better.

"Anything on him from your FBI snitches?"

"No. I could ask, but that would cost you. You want to run a tab?" asked Geier.

This told him that the informants worked on a per-job basis, not on retainer. Vivian would want him to say yes, so she could watch bank accounts, and target the snitches. But he preferred to not get caught.

From outside there was an indistinct yell and the bell abruptly quit ringing.

"No thanks," said Shark. "I've barely got the territory in the black. I can't run any tabs. I'll figure out what he wants and deal with him."

Geier laughed. "You're the oldest young person I know. So conservative with your cash. Next thing you know, you'll be drinking Metamucil and yelling at children."

"Stay the fuck off my lawn," agreed Shark.

Thursday ~ December 8

Shark: The Police Station

Shark saw Vivian's number flash on his phone and ignored it, preferring to finish putting away his groceries. When she called again seconds later, he grudgingly picked up. "Yeah?"

"I just got the courtesy call," she said without preamble. "They're on their way to arrest you. If you're carrying, ditch it. I'm on my way."

Shark hung up and began unbuckling his belt with one hand, dialing Marko with the other.

"I'm about to be arrested," he said when Marko picked up.

"Shit."

"Do we have a lawyer that's even in this zip code?" he asked, working the holster off his belt. He hurried into the bedroom to put the gun into the wall safe behind the mirror.

"Uh..." Marko was stalled. "No? Shit."

"OK, that sucks. Ask the Fives for a recommendation. If you can't get anyone in the next ten minutes, call Peri, get her to give you a referral. I'll call you when they give me my phone call."

"Right. Good luck." Marko hung up.

Shark put the phone in the wall safe, locked it. There were a number of other guns hidden around the place. It wouldn't withstand a true search, but it would withstand a cursory once-over. He didn't have time to do more than that. Hopefully, Vivian could stall them. He pulled on his coat and went down to wait by his car. If they arrested him outside the condo, it might discourage them from searching it.

His parking lot and condo looked out over a man-made reservoir pond surrounded by tall grasses that poked brown tips sadly through the crust of snow. At the moment, the water was half-frozen and looked blurry as if it were out of focus. Until living in the suburbs, Shark had not known that water did that.

As the cops pulled in, he pretended to be about to get in his car. But they took too long to get through the crusted ruts of ice at the parking lot entrance and he had to give up and just wait. They were flustered by the time they got to him and compensated by pinching the cuffs extra tight. Shark missed the professionalism of the city where the cops would have either kneed him in the balls for being witness to their embarrassment or joked about their inability to drive. Mildly numb fingers seemed like half-assed retribution.

He was being charged with selling liquor to minors. He hadn't actually worked the cash register on any of the nights the bowling alley had been open, so it seemed like a trumped-up charge. When he saw Agent Fowler at the station he knew it was. When they moved him into an interrogation room instead of directly into processing, he knew he'd be out within twenty-four hours.

Shark settled into the lightly padded seat at the metal table and admired how clean the interrogation room was. The suburbs really knew how to roll out the red carpet. The table barely had any dicks drawn on it. Out of curiosity, he checked the underside for gum. Except for the COPS ARE COCKSUCKERS scratched vertically down one leg, it was practically pristine.

A vice cop came in and yelled at him for a while. When he finally paused for a breath, Shark turned to the camera placed on the wall above the two-way mirror and said, "I'm invoking my right to counsel. I want a lawyer."

He waited until that cop left and then stretched. Waiting was always the worst part about being arrested. He patted his pockets looking for a paperclip to add his own graffiti, but then decided he was probably too old for that. He felt a pang of nostalgia for the days when he could scratch swear words onto all police owned items without worrying about his reputation. He'd once spray painted the back end of a squad car with ASK ME ABOUT FREE BLOW JOBS. And he was pretty sure the giant dick he'd carved into the two-way mirror down at the eighty-first street precinct was still there.

A second cop walked in with a cup of crappy police station coffee. His m.o. was being reasonable and genuine. Shark took a sip of the coffee because, why not? Then he simply said, "Lawyer," and handed the coffee back to him.

A few hours later he was bored, hungry, thirsty, and tired of listening to cops. None of the questions were about the charge he'd been arrested for. Instead, they were all nosing around the sudden disappearance of Big Paulie. The questions were vague enough that he'd immediately ceased to worry. They didn't have anything.

Finally, around five, Agent Fowler walked in. Shark watched as he reached up and turned off the camera.

Without the bustle of the bowling alley to distract him, he was able to see that Fowler's pot belly was covering muscle, and the ill-fitting suit wasn't necessarily cheap, just loose enough to cover shoulder and ankle holsters. The man needed a tailor, but the suit wasn't as bad as it first appeared. There was no accounting for his taste in ties though.

Shark checked his watch. "I was beginning to think you weren't going to show. You know, if you wanted a meeting, you could have just stopped by the bowling alley."

Fowler punched him. Shark had expected it. Why else turn off the camera? Didn't mean it didn't sting like a son of a bitch.

"I call the meetings," said Fowler with a nasty smile. Shark could see that he'd been bleaching his teeth. The tan though, was that spray-on or real?

"Yes, I hear you had several meetings with Big Paulie," said Shark. "You know, it would seem unnecessary for us to have this much friction. I think we should be able to work things out like gentlemen."

Fowler hit him again. "I don't have to be a gentleman." He leaned down until he was inches away from Shark's face. Shark noticed his pupils were widely dilated and the white areas were red.

"I'm the boss," hissed Fowler. "Get it through your head."

He began tapping on Shark's temple. "You can't move in on my action. We're going to do this my way."

A narcissistic cokehead. Great. Just what he wanted for Christmas.

Shark leaned away from the poking finger and considered his options. "And what is your way? Just so I'm clear."

For a moment, Fowler seemed to think, then his mood shifted. "Oh, you'd like that, wouldn't you?" he said, sniffing and standing up straight. "I'm not telling you shit. I heard about you. You and Geier go way back. You're all tight and shit. Well, I'm going to take your territory and Geier can go fuck himself. Clear out of the bowling alley, or I'll shut you down for good."

He faked a punch, then laughed even though Shark hadn't flinched. He switched the camera back on and left the room laughing.

Moments later a youngish blonde guy in a stylish winter coat and suit combo came in with Vivian. Her eyes widened slightly when she saw his split lip. The young man smiled.

"Mr. Santoyo, I'm Taylor Williamson. I'm your lawyer."

That explained the smile. Lawyers loved it when their clients got beaten. It was so much leverage all in one tidy picture.

Shark: Outside the Police Station

Shark had to admit, Taylor Williamson threw a truly elegant hissy fit. There were multi-syllable words, waving of papers, subtle accusations of racism, and a truly stinging indictment of their coffee. Shark appreciated the last one the most. He wasn't sure how it tied in, but he liked that it was there.

In the end, Williamson got his way and Shark was released without charges. Vivian gave him a stern warning to make his next appointment, but didn't follow him out of the station. Williamson led him out the front door, where Marko was waiting in the loading zone of the slushy parking lot, leaning against his car as if daring a police officer to say something.

Shark slid his sunglasses on and took a tiny moment to revel in the triumph, surveying his surroundings. It was hard to take suburban policing seriously. The parking lot had damn Christmas banners up. On the curb, there was a recycling bin for holiday lights next to an even larger bin for a canned food drive. In the city the canned food box would have been robbed and the entire light container would probably have been stolen or set on fire.

"Were all the detectives gnomes or some shit? This place is like the fucking Disneyland of police stations," said Marko, as they reached the bottom of the stairs, walking carefully over the gritty salt and layers of ice.

"No, but I think I saw a cartoon bluebird flying by when Fowler punched me," said Shark. Marko snorted.

"Shark! Hey! Shark!"

They all turned to see who was bellowing Shark's name and saw two officers manhandling a staggering biker in green colors into the station. Shark recognized the Vagos patch and after a moment he recognized Mateo through his long hair.

"Hey Shark," slurred Mateo, *"¿Cómo está tu novia?"* He followed this up with a kissing noise. One of the officers shoved Mateo forward, and Shark turned back without acknowledging the question.

"Who's that dipshit?" asked Marko, giving Mateo a hard stare.

"A Vagos who doesn't like my driving."

"Well, it probably doesn't need to be said, but he's exactly the kind of person I recommend you not associate with," said Williamson.

"I couldn't agree more." Shark held out his hand.

"Glad it was such a clear-cut case of police misconduct. Let me know if you want to sue. And take pictures of your face. You may want that evidence later."

Shark nodded. "Thanks for the advice. What do we owe you?"

"Oh, not to worry," said Williamson. "I'll invoice you. Marko gave me the address." With a cheerful wave he walked off, bee-lining for a green, snub-nosed Smart Car.

"Good lawyer," said Shark. "But…"

"Little light in the loafers?" asked Marko, raising an eyebrow. "Yeah, Eddie was embarrassed to give me the name, but swears he's the best."

"Hey, we're an open mob," said Shark.

"I just didn't realize we were that open," said Marko grinning. "Meanwhile, my Spanish may be piss poor, but I don't think that Vagos said anything about driving. Something about a girlfriend?"

Shark shrugged. He'd been hoping Marko wouldn't notice that. As usual, Marko was smarter than he looked.

"You got a girlfriend I don't know about, or was he just shitting on Williamson? Because you could totally get a Williamson."

Shark snorted. "He means Peri. There was a thing at this bar a few months back when I was dealing with the Abernathy situation. We may have ended up on his bad side." He spread his hands, giving up. "What are you going to do?"

"Watch your back," suggested Marko, pushing away from the car and opening the passenger door for Shark. "Vagos are fucking bad news."

Shark got into Marko's Benz and waited for him to start the car. "Where are we at on Fowler?"

"The basics. Home, work addresses. Ex-wife moved to Arizona five years ago. No other family. No pets. Girlfriend appears to be his hand and some regular hookers."

"So, the same place we were a week ago?" Shark was annoyed.

"Just about, yeah."

"OK, time to get serious. Send Beef or Eddie to go talk to

the hookers. Keep it on the downlow. I don't want him knowing that we've been asking around. Meanwhile, pick out a couple of the kids who know the meaning of the word discreet and start tailing him. I want to know if he so much as scratches his ass. Fowler's threatening to push us out of the territory and I'm not about to let some blowjob screw this up for me."

"Cokehead?"

"Judging by the red eyes and constant sniffing, yeah."

"We should find his dealer, then," said Marko.

"That would be nice."

Monday ~ December 26, Boxing Day

Peregrine: Under the Overpass

The sky was stark white and the first few flakes of snow were hitting the ground as Peri scrambled up the support strut of the overpass near mile marker forty. Hanging on by her fingertips, she felt into the nook above her head, groping for the camera she'd placed there the week before. Her left hand throbbed under her gloves from the dog bite. Like everything else that had happened over Christmas, the wound in her palm aggravated her even as she tried to ignore it. A pigeon flapped angrily at her and she dropped back down, forced to admit that the camera was no longer there.

She attempted to dust off her gloves, but realized the dirt was not going anywhere and used the back of her hand to brush a strand of wavy dark-chocolate-colored hair out of her eyes. She scanned the scrub grass and accumulated drifts of trash. She'd lost one camera already when the vibrations of the cars overhead bounced it out of her hidey hole.

She scanned the ground. No broken plastic or glass.

"Looking for your camera?" boomed a voice.

Two men were walking toward her. One was pushing a shopping cart full of scrap metal and a reel of copper wire. They were filthy, bearded, and one had open sores on his face. She could smell them from where she stood. "Found it yesterday. Pawned it." He seemed smug.

Peri sighed. "And I don't suppose you remember where?"

"Fuck you!" said the other one. "Who do you think you are? We own this turf! We get all the metal!"

Peri sighed again. "I don't give a shit about you," she said honestly. "Tell me where you pawned it and I'll give you twenty bucks."

"How about you give me a hand job and I'll think about it," said the first one, leering.

Peri checked her phone. Her Lyft was almost here. She did not have time for this shit.

"How about you tell me where you pawned it and I won't break your arm?" she suggested. The second man flung a chunk of metal at her. She caught it one-handed and threw it back. It bounced off his face and he dropped like a rock. The first guy looked stunned.

"I don't actually want to touch you," she told him, walking over. "I don't want MRSA or whatever. Just tell me where you pawned it and I won't have to hurt you."

He took a swing at her. She blocked and punched him in the gut. He gagged and swung with the other hand. She blocked again, grabbed his wrist and twisted it. He sagged to his knees trying to relieve the pressure.

"Where is it?"

"Fuck you!"

She twisted harder.

"I don't remember!"

Her Lyft pulled up. The bum took her moment of distraction to attempt to spit at her, but she heard the loogie forming and punched him. The combination of force and spin knocked him out. At five foot four inches and 115 pounds, she generally wasn't strong enough to get knockouts from single punches.

"Badass," said the Lyft driver, rolling down his window. Peri wanted to agree with him, but nothing made you look less cool than liking your own posts, so she shrugged.

"Hey Otto," she said, climbing into the passenger seat.

"Hey Peri." Otto clicked his app. "Why I always pick you up in the strange places?"

Peri could have told him that it was because her "afterschool job" was as a fixer for the teenage crime set, but that always got awkward. For one thing, adults never believed there was a teenage crime set. "I enjoy geocaching," she told him.

Otto rolled his eyes. "Full contact geocaching?" he asked and Peri laughed. "Seriously, why you fight so good?"

In most cases she would have responded with a simple *fuck off*. But Otto was one of her preferred Lyft drivers. He wanted to import his family from Europe, and he *didn't* want to work for the Ukrainian mob, which meant that, since she tipped well, he didn't mind driving to the aforementioned strange places. So, for Otto she selected an honest, if edited, answer.

"My uncle was in the Marines. I train with him." She didn't add that her uncle was ex-Marine Force Recon and she was now a full member at his gym—a small low-rent dive that could have been featured heavily in *Cauliflower Ear Quarterly*.

"Huh," he said in response. "How was your Christmas?"

"My boyfriend moved to California. My mom made us have Christmas with *her* boyfriend. I'm pretty sure my uncle went on an alcoholic bender and that's why he won't call me back. And the guy I like hasn't called in, like, months," said Peri. "How was yours?"

"I talked to my mom. She said her brother was put in prison for publishing an article that criticized the regime. My niece wants to marry a Turkish guy and convert to Islam, so her father beat her pretty bad and he got arrested. And my wife says they've run out of gas for the generator, which means they don't have any heat, and they can't buy more until next week."

"So you're saying my Christmas was pretty good?"

"Could have been worse," said Otto.

Shark: Rolling Thunder Lanes

Shark drummed his fingers on the bar. The man in front of him smirked confidently. He was a paunchy forty-something white guy that maybe used to be in shape, but hadn't quite realized that he wasn't anymore. Paper and Marko had brought him in.

At the last meeting when Beef had mentioned the shakedown he gave the girls on the street, Paper had looked thoughtful. Now, Shark knew why. Paper had skipped the hos and gone directly to their pimp—one of his regular customers. Shark walked around the bar leaving his Jack and Coke. Paper and Marko were lounging in the background, leaning on the railing between the lanes and bar area. Domingo, Beef, and Eddie were playing cards at one of the tables. The game was sucking because they were mostly watching the action between Shark and the guy in front of him.

"I think this is worth five hundred," said the guy with a grin. "You want Fowler and I can tell you where he'll be. I can give him to you on a platter."

"What's your name again?"

"It doesn't matter what my name is," said the guy, looking around, like he was expecting Marko and Paper to join him in laughing. "Just give me the cash and I can tell you what you want to know."

"Why?"

"Why? You think I give a shit about law enforcement? Tanisha has been banging him for like a year. Does he ever tip extra? Does he ever feed her? No. Half the time he tries to stiff her and pass off some shitty black hearts as payment. Fuck that guy. Just pay me the cash and we can all get what we want."

"I meant, why would I pay you?" asked Shark, circling the man slowly. This guy reminded him of every asshole who had ever tried to short him when he used to work the street corner. It hadn't worked when he was fifteen and it certainly wasn't going to work now.

The pimp twisted to follow Shark's movements. "I got what you need."

"You're going to give me that anyway," said Shark. "If Paper wants to, maybe he'll give you something to go home on."

"Kid," said the pimp. "Don't try to kid a kidder. Stop fronting big and do business."

"What's this guy's name again?" he asked, turning back to Paper.

"Ralph," said Paper. "Most people call him Squirrel though. They say he fucked a squirrel to death."

"I guess his dick is tiny," said Marko. "Otherwise, I don't see how that's possible."

"You want to measure?" demanded Ralph, grabbing his groin. Neither Marko or Paper moved.

"Paper says you're a regular customer," said Shark, circling again. "Tell me what I want and I'll give you this week's for free."

"That's not a deal," said the guy, laughing, and flexing his shoulders a little as to subtly display how much he outweighed Shark. "I'm walking out of here with paper money."

Shark punched him. Ralph grunted; Shark hit him again, this time targeting the kidney. Ralph doubled over and Shark kneed him in the face. Ralph staggered back, tripped and tried to catch himself on the barstool.

"Ralph," Shark said, pausing to take a sip of his drink, "you're going to tell me what I want to know. You can tell me now, or you can tell me twenty minutes from now when I start breaking bones."

"Come on, man," he gasped, hauling himself to his feet. "Be reasonable."

"This *is* me being reasonable," said Shark calmly.

"They said you were nice to your guys," protested Ralph.

"You're not my guy." Shark hit him again. Then he grabbed him by the hair and slammed his face into the bar—a tooth went shooting out along the dark oak.

Shark released him and he fell backward onto the floor. He looked semi-conscious at best. Paper grabbed a pitcher of water off the bar and poured it over him. Ralph spluttered and coughed.

"Tell me what you know," said Shark, "and you can walk out right now."

Ralph rolled onto his side, coughing up blood and water. "Sacred Heart, eleven-thirty on Wednesday."

"OK," said Shark. "Great. You can leave now."

The rest of the room watched Ralph rise with difficulty. He looked for a moment like he might say something else, but then he limped from the room.

"This is going to be a problem for us," said Domingo when the door closed.

"You think Paper can't handle the squirrel fucker?" asked Shark, picking up his drink.

"That is not what I meant!" said Domingo, turning to Paper and holding up his hands.

Shark didn't think that was what Domingo meant, but it was what Geier would have said. Geier liked to sow discord among the ranks. It kept people on their toes.

"Then what's the problem?" demanded Shark. Ralph saying that he was nice had irked him.

"Sacred Heart is an all-girl's school," said Domingo.

Peregrine: The Unicorn Graveyard

Peri tried to focus on what Trey was saying. Trey usually had solid, supportive things to say, as befit the perfect boyfriend. Trey was a straight-*A* student, had adorable dimples, perfectly smooth, dark-brown skin, and he believed in feminism, environmentalism, and the sanctity of Monday Night Football. And right now, he was annoying the shit out of her.

She dangled, face down, off the side of the bed and realized that her pink bedside area rug was literally threadbare—the weft of the carpet was showing through in the places she most commonly placed her feet. She was aware that in her role as *normal teenage girl* she should redecorate away from her junior high color scheme, but, much to her mother's distress, her bedroom décor never made it anywhere near the top of her priority list. She considered the rug again. A new rug would be nice, but full on redecorating would be such a pain in the ass—she'd have to figure out all new hiding places for her weapons. Her phone vibrated annoyingly against her cheek to alert her of an incoming text.

She rolled over on her ancient purple bedspread and switched to speaker, so she could look at the message.

It's Shark. Can we meet?

Peri stared at the phone. And then glanced up, as if for advice, to the shelf full of stuffed animals above her bed. Dilapidated

Winky Pegasus offered no comments. *Can we meet?* What was that supposed to mean?

"I don't know," continued Trey, unaware of her divided attention. "It sounds like Rodney was making an effort. Maybe you should cut him some slack."

Peri blinked, re-focusing on Trey's voice. And how was she supposed to respond to that? Telling her boyfriend to fuck off probably wasn't going to go well. "Um, I'll think about it."

Trey laughed. "Meaning, you're not going to think about it. Anyway, sounds like your Christmas was mostly pretty good."

Mostly pretty good? Had he not listened to anything she said?

"Christmas out here was OK too."

Trey continued to talk as she composed.

Last time *you* texted me, I ended up having to borrow your sweats.

And stabbing a guy in the eyeball, but she wasn't about to put that in text.

"I mean, I missed my mom. But at least no one in my cousin's family got drunk and threw things at my head like Uncle Jimmy." Trey's mom was barely in the ground and his drug-dealing, as-shat Uncle Jimmy's body was still in the morgue as evidence in the drive-by shooting that ended his life. For Trey, simply having someone *not* throw things at him was a step up.

"Sounds lovely," said Peri, retreating into the tone she reserved for her mom, full of false cheer and only occasional bitter notes as a new message popped through.

Fair point. Test question?

Shark was always so reasonable. It was one of the reasons

she liked him so much. She considered possible questions, trying to pinpoint something that only he would know.

WHAT KIND OF UNDERWEAR DO I WEAR?

"Frank, that's my cousin's husband, smoked a turkey. That was weird. But he let me help. It tasted good."

Peri stared at the phone, caught by the tone in Trey's voice. He sounded… OK. And that was new, because he hadn't been OK in a long time. Peri ran her hand through her hair and felt guilty about the wave of relief that was washing over her. That had been the goal, right? To make everything OK for Trey.

PINEAPPLES.

Considering that the pineapple-print underwear were the only pair of her panties Shark had seen, it was a safe answer.

She had started a minor gang war, robbed a drug stash house, and orchestrated a drive-by shooting all to secure a safe, normal, happy future for Trey, and she'd succeeded. She should be happy for him. She was happy for him. She was also relieved. Relieved to no longer have to work so hard to hide her extra-curricular activities. Relieved to no longer be responsible for his happiness. Relieved to have the weight of him off her shoulders. Relieved that he was gone. And that felt awful, because she loved him.

And also, she was talking to another guy about her underwear. It was possible that she was a horrible, horrible girlfriend. "Hey Trey, I just got some weird text from my mom. I'm going to have to call you back."

"Oh. Sure. I've got to go anyway. They have some tradition about going out for Chinese food the day after Christmas anyway."

"Cool. OK, call you later. Love you!"

"Love you too!"

Peri cut off the call and switched to texting. WHERE AND WHEN?

TONIGHT. LOCATION AND TIME YOUR CALL.

Classic Shark—always sure to give her options so she felt safe.

I WAS GOING TO DO DINNER AT THE THAI PLACE ON SPRUCE. MEET YOU THERE AT SIX? DO I NEED TO BRING ANY EQUIPMENT?

NO EQUIPMENT. TALK ONLY. SEE YOU THEN.

"Talk only," she said to the unicorn poster on the wall. She should probably get a new poster as well as a new rug.

Talk only sounded like no making out.

Posters all seemed so juvenile. Maybe she could get some real art? There had been a fascinating Paul Soldner mixed media piece that she'd seen in a gallery window over Christmas. But she didn't think a three-thousand-dollar mid-century modern painting said eighteen-year-old adultish girl any more than a cartoon unicorn did. But she couldn't just take it down either—she had to have something in that spot to cover the space she'd cut into the wall. She stored all of the emergency kits she gave to girls there—she couldn't let her mom see those. Bulk supplies of Plan B and condoms could give a parent the wrong impression.

Talk only sounded like work.

And what was she supposed to do about her unicorn storage system? She looked up at Winky Pegasus again. He really did look sad. Of course, being hollowed out and used to store illicit substances generally had that effect on a stuffed animal.

Talk only sounded like she was going to need to look extra cute.

It was moments like this that she missed having a best friend. She should be on the phone now working out an outfit, planning strategy. Instinctively she looked at the picture of Vicki on her dresser. Vicki was sticking her tongue out, and behind them Trey held up bunny ears over their heads. Peri's younger self grinned manically, clinging to Vicki. Peri looked out the window. As usual, she was on her own.

Shark: That Thai Place on 38th

They both arrived twenty minutes early and saw each other coming from opposite ends of the alley behind the restaurant. There was the awkward moment of silence while they both struggled with whether or not to acknowledge that they were scoping the place for traps.

"For the future, we could agree that if it's just us, we go ahead and arrive at the actual time given," suggested Shark.

Peri looked like she was considering it. "That doesn't sound like us."

He conceded her point with a nod of his head and a ghost of a smile. "It's good to see you."

"Good to see you, too," said Peri, almost smiling back at him. "Now let's go inside. I ended up walking and I'm freezing my knees off."

He looked over her winter-cute outfit of sweater, leggings and puffy jacket. "You could have worn more than tights," he said. "You do know those aren't real pants, right?"

"And you need a haircut."

He ran his hand through his hair self-consciously. Did she hate it? When they'd met a few months ago it had been short. "I'm scared to try a place out here and I keep forgetting when I'm in the city."

"This is the suburbs, not the outer reaches of Mongolia. We do have people who can cut hair."

He held the door open for her. "You say that now. But then I show up with my fade all sideways and you'd be embarrassed to be seen with me." He didn't add that one of the reasons he hated the suburbs was that he felt cut off from his network. In the city, he could list three barbers off the top of his head and, if he was desperate, a simple text would get him a recommendation for three more. It wasn't about the barber—it was the fact that he lacked a basic level of knowledge. She, more than most people, would understand that, but he didn't care to expose the weakness.

"Yes," she said, her eyes twinkling, looking back over her shoulder, "because your hair is what I worry about when I'm with you." He grinned and stamped his boots on the front mat.

"Two?" asked the host, looking at the pair of them. Shark thought he looked surprised.

"Yes," said Shark. "And can we have the table furthest from the door."

"Yes, of course." There was something in the host's tone that suggested that it was strange he'd even asked. As the host gave him a careful once over, Shark wondered how often Peri came here. If it was often, he didn't think she came here with anyone—the host was too interested.

She took the seat facing the door. Shark sat opposite and by the time they'd heard the specials and gotten water he'd already spent more time checking the room than looking at the menu.

"How was your Christmas?" he asked.

Peri's expression would have turned steam to snowflakes. "I think we can skip my Christmas."

"Not with that face. The face says it was epic. I want the dirt." Unable to help himself, he looked over his shoulder again.

Peri clunked her water glass on the table. "Only if you move over to my side. You're going to break your neck trying to keep an eye on everyone."

"I don't like sitting with my back to the room," he complained.

"Neither do I. Just move, so I can stop talking to the back of your head."

"Not being a very good date, am I?" He pushed his glass and menu across the table before moving beside her. "Is this better?"

"Yeah, now I can talk to your ear."

He laughed and angled his chair slightly. On this side of the table he was a lot closer to her and as his knee knocked against hers, he realized his tactical error. He was supposed to be keeping his distance. On the other hand, she didn't appear to be worried, or even particularly happy to see him. Her Christmas must have sucked donkey balls to put her in this kind of mood. He thought about trying to say something to put her in a more charitable frame of mind and then realized who he was talking to. He didn't need to sweet- talk Peri. That would only annoy her further. "OK, spill," he said. "You're grumpy as hell. What happened?"

She angled her chair to face his, creating some distance, and settled back against her puffy jacket.

"It's not that big of a deal," she hedged. "But Mom wanted us to spend Christmas with Rodney—the boyfriend." He made the appropriate grimace. "So, we went up to the city. His apartment was all…" she hesitated, looking for the right word, "neutral. Like all beige and white and cream. Very tasteful, if you have no taste."

"White people style."

"I'd be offended if that weren't true. Anyway, I felt like I couldn't sit anywhere and he's got a yappy little dog. It was all annoying, but I was committed, so I tried to be cool. And then for Christmas he gives me one of those fucking expensive charm bracelets with all the weird clunky beads."

Shark rubbed the scar on his eyebrow and tried to figure out what would cause a person to buy Peri a gift like that. There was no logic in it. Was the mom's boyfriend delusional or just monumentally stupid?

"Is that disbelief or are you unfamiliar with the hideousness?" she asked, checking his expression.

"I'm familiar," he said, taking a sip of water. "I'm just trying to picture a piece of jewelry that you would like less. It's both figuratively and literally loud. It gives away far too much personal information. And, what are you, a middle-aged woman?"

"Yes!" gasped Peri, sitting up straight. "Yes, to that! To all of that! Thank you!" She slumped back in her chair exhaling her relief. "Finally, someone understands."

"It's weird, but hardly disastrous," he said, smiling. He felt like he was getting bonus points off the inadequacy of others.

"And maybe if that had been it, I would have been fine."

"What happened next?"

"So now it's Christmas evening. He had dinner catered,

because that's stock broker takeout? It went OK. Then I excused myself to go to the restroom and I come back and they are making out like mad. And if that weren't my mom I'd be more inclined to wish them well. But she is, so ew. So, I go back out in the hall and I make some noise, and go back in. They're still going at it. I finally yelled that I was going out for a soda and I left. I ended up walking around and looking at art galleries and Christmas lights."

Shark chuckled.

"Laugh it up. That's not the worst."

"What happened next?"

"This morning I'm finally making headway with the yappy little Mini Pinscher. I'm sitting on the couch and it's smelling my hand. Then my mom said something and I looked away."

"Mistake?"

"Yeah. Because then it bit me."

His eyes flew to her hand and he realized what he had assumed to be the sleeve of her shirt trailing out of her sweater was actually a bandage. He stopped smiling and held out his hand. She put her hand into his and he peeled back the strip of gauze to look at the puncture marks in the heel of her palm.

"What'd you do?" he asked, examining the mark. It probably stung like a mother, but it wasn't bad. The dog must have indeed been tiny. But he was not amused. Her mother should take better care of her. And possibly Rodney should have it explained to him that Peri was not to be damaged. He realized that she hadn't answered his question and looked up at her. She was watching his inspection of her hand with a serious expression.

"I punched it," she said, and his shoulders convulsed in laughter. Peri's lips twitched. "It was an instinctive reaction!"

"Dog puncher!" He said, laughing harder, but keeping hold of her hand.

"It did kind of fly across the room. Then mom yelled at me for punching the dog and he's yelling at me for bleeding on his couch. It's Italian leather! It's handcrafted!"

Chuckling, he rewrapped the bandage and tucked it securely into place.

"Uncomfortable is what that couch is. Anyway, I faked getting a text from my lab partner. Our project was about to tank, blah blah blah. Then I hopped on a train and came home. And that was my shitty-ass Christmas. How'd yours go?"

"Slept in. Watched a Christmas parade on TV. Marko came over and made some sort of delicious French thing I can't pronounce and then we sat around, drank beer and watched two *Die Hards* and a *Lethal Weapon*."

Peri stared at him as if he'd announced that he'd taken a blimp ride.

"Are you in disbelief or are you unfamiliar with the work of John McClane?" he asked.

Peri opened and closed her mouth a few times. Her hands made nebulous circles in front of her. "My jealousy is so overwhelming right now that I'm having a hard time processing."

"Sorry," he said. "Maybe New Year's will be better?"

"Not unless Rodney accidentally gets hit by a car."

"I can probably make that happen," he offered.

"Don't even think about it!"

"Why not? I think I probably owe you for the thing at the bowling alley."

"Yes, and seeing how that turned out, I obviously shouldn't have interfered. How's that going for you anyway?"

"It's why I called, actually," he said. "I have an idea and I need your help."

Peri sat up straighter, showing more enthusiasm than she had since they had arrived. He felt a pang of inadequacy. Did she really like him or did she just like the work?

"Hey Peri," said the server, a fiftyish mom type, confirming his theory that Peri ate here often enough that this was her table. The waitress gave Shark the once-over, clocked his expensive jacket and watch, and smiled at Peri. "Let me guess, you want a green curry with chicken."

"I'm going out on a limb tonight, Sue. Give me a red curry with beef."

"Way to change it up. What can I get you, hon?" She turned Shark with a smile.

"I'll have the special," he said. Shark turned back to face Peri, who looked like she was trying not to laugh. Shark glanced suspiciously at Sue, but didn't say anything as the waitress bustled away.

"The last I heard was from Domingo, the day after," said Peri. "He gave me the bump and pass in the hallway—shoved a note at me. Said it was the ATF investigating. No calls. No visits."

Shark nodded. He'd told Domingo to warn her off. The last thing he needed was for her to get spotted by Vivian or Fowler.

"So the douchebag was actually ATF, not FBI? Sorry if I got him all riled up."

Shark shook his head. "He was going to be on my ass no matter what. Agent Fowler and Big Paulie had some sort of off the books business arrangement. And now that I've, uh, replaced Big Paulie, he is extremely aggravated and wants me out."

"Jeez, Big Paulie is the gift that won't stop giving," said Peri. Considering that Big Paulie's business partner had almost killed both of them, Peri had no love for the deceased territory boss. "What was his arrangement with Big Paulie?"

"That's the worst part," said Shark. "I don't know. And at this point I don't think it matters. He's looking to take me and the rest of the boys out of the equation. He's got the cops pushing on us at every turn. Right now, opening the bowling alley as a legit business is looking like the smartest thing I ever did. It's the only thing that's protecting us."

Peri frowned. "Well, not to advocate short cuts, but can't you just, you know... take care of him?"

He smiled at her. He did love that she wasn't squeamish about pretty much any aspect of his business. It made talking to her so much simpler.

"At this point, no. If he showed up with so much as a hangnail, scratched bumper, or burglary, I'd get hauled in. Everyone in the state knows that he's investigating me."

"So what are you going to do?"

"I'm going to catch him," said Shark confidently. Peri raised an eyebrow. "If he won't leave crime to the criminals, then I don't see why I have to leave policing to the cops. I'll find whatever it is that he's afraid I've got, or I'll dig up something new, and I'm going to make sure he gets busted. We'll see how he likes prison from the inside."

Peri laughed. "OK, blue blood, what's the plan?"

"I've got the guys going through Big Paulie's papers. I don't have a lot of hopes for that. Reading is not their strong suit, and record keeping wasn't Paulie's. So mostly I'm focusing on Fowler. I had the guys looking into his life. Marko shook down his favorite hookers, but that didn't get us anything."

"I have a hard time with hookers," said Peri, nodding sympathetically. She looked up and Shark tried to maintain a poker face. "What?"

"You question hookers a lot, do you?"

"More than you'd think," said Peri defensively. "And they either think I'm trying to move in on their action or I'm trying to Bible-belt them. It takes me forever to get anything useful."

"Ah, I see your point. I imagine we do have the advantage on you in that department. Tell you what, next time you need a hooker questioned you can borrow Marko."

"You don't need to make fun of me!" she protested, blushing.

"I wouldn't dream of it," he said, although he knew his smile said differently. Reaching out, he pulled a loose hair off her sweater. He recognized the gesture for what it was—a reason to touch her. He really was going to have to put a stop to that. At least she didn't seem to be having problems with keeping things on point. He didn't want to have to actually say anything. That was a conversation that would suck and he needed her to keep working with him.

"I was being serious," he said. "You can borrow Marko if you need him. He's good at it. Anyway, your hooker problems aside, we've run down about every inch of this guy's life. The one person I can't find is his dealer. Which makes me suspicious."

"Could he be getting it in the city?" suggested Peri.

Shark shrugged. "Doesn't matter at this point. We've wasted a lot of time and gotten nowhere. We've got to start moving. That's where you come in. There's a laptop he takes almost everywhere with him. We can't get near him at work, but we've identified a potential opening."

"You want me to steal it?"

"I want you to upload malware. If we can backdoor his computer, then either we can find evidence or we can plant evidence. Either way, we win."

Peri nodded. "Well within my skill set. Seems like a decent idea and totally possible. When and where?"

"That's the tricky part. Fowler is giving a high school career talk on Wednesday."

"What do you need me for, then?" she asked. "Just have Domingo or one of the other kids from the crew do it."

"The talk is at Sacred Heart."

Peri laughed. "And you don't think Domingo would look that great in knee-highs and a plaid skirt."

"He's probably got the legs for it," said Shark, "but I'm not sure he's comfortable with non-conforming gender roles. Do you have the time?"

"Time's not the problem," said Peri with a shrug. "The bigger problem is the location."

"Well, I know it's not your high school, but can you do it?"

Peri fiddled with the end of her braid and looked like she was considering the problem. Sue arrived with their order. "Do you want me to put in your takeout order now?" she asked, carefully putting down the brimming bowl full of curry.

"Yes, please. And can you put in some of the black sticky rice?"

"Sure thing," said Sue.

"Takeout order?" asked Shark and Peri grimaced like she wished she hadn't said it. Shark understood the problem. It was too easy to feel comfortable talking to Peri and end up saying more than he should. It made him feel a little better that she had the same problem.

"I usually order extra for Mom. That way we don't have to cook tomorrow, or she's got something to eat if she comes home early."

There wasn't any reason for her to lie, and she didn't have a tell—but his instinct said it wasn't true.

"Anyway, yeah, I can do it," she said, casually changing the topic to cover her slip. "Sacred Heart's a little more complex, but I can handle it."

"Cool," said Shark. He supposed that he could push harder to find out the truth, but her business was her business. He liked and respected her, but it wasn't as if he trusted her with all of his secrets either. He had no intention of making that mistake again.

Peregrine: In His Car

Peri nestled the takeout securely into the floor area behind the passenger seat. Shark watched the process with a critical eye.

"It won't spill on your precious car," she said. "Promise."

"I didn't say anything!"

"You were thinking thoughts," she said turning around and buckling into her seat.

"I admit I may have been thinking about how you'd look cleaning my car."

"I'd look like I was paying for detailing," she said.

"So boss," he said, shaking his head.

She tried not to giggle. He always turned her into such a girly-girl. She shouldn't have let him pay for the takeout. She felt like it crossed some sort of boundary. But he'd just handled the bill so smoothly it was done before she could object. She didn't have enough practice at that kind of thing. Everyone she ate with split the bill religiously. It was just more evidence that Shark was out of her league in so many ways, but when he smiled at her... Peri fought the urge to melt in her boots.

He started the car. "OK," he said, continuing the previous conversation. "I know the timeline is a little tight. What do you need to make it happen?"

"I got it. Don't worry about it." He gave her a look and this time Peri did laugh. "Yes, I know. It's your job to worry. Worrying is what you do. But in this instance, I can take care of gathering all the supplies and setting up my access to the target. If you can arrange my delivery and exit, then we'll be OK."

He looked unconvinced and Peri realized that she was staring at his eyes, which were undeniably gorgeous, fringed with miles of eyelashes, and well worth staring into, but that did not do a lot to bolster her reputation as tough and sensible.

"Remember, you're hiring a consultant for a reason. This is a full-service corporation, which, of course, will be reflected in your bill. But, you *do* get what you pay for."

"Yeah, but don't you need a uniform or some shit? Can you just wave your magic wand and make that appear?"

Peri thought about that. There were some obstacles. Her main contact at Sacred Heart—a bubbly auburn-haired cutie named Sarah Pearson who was a solid pickpocket and good at running interference—had graduated last year. Then there was the fact that her old uniform was no longer viable due to an incident involving marinara sauce and Sarah's younger sister, Hannah. She was going to have to move quickly to do some bridge-building at Sacred Heart and get a replacement uniform in time. But on the other hand, other than hitting pawn shops looking for the missing camera, what else was she doing with her week?

"Well, as far as you need to know it's snap," she said. "Don't worry about it."

This time he laughed, and the worried expression eased up.

"OK, well, meet up tomorrow at the bowling alley and we'll go over the plans. Make sure we got everything."

Her house was less than a mile away and he pulled up at her driveway far too soon. She took out her gloves, preparing for the trek up the walk. "You want to come in?" she asked, aiming for casual, as she reached into the back for her takeout.

"Peri," he began, trying to make eye contact around the bag. His face had an uncomfortable, serious expression which promptly produced knots in her stomach. He pushed the containers down toward her feet impatiently. "About last time…"

She felt a clammy rush of adrenaline and anger. God, he was being so awkward. Just say it. He didn't like her *that* way.

"Last time, we got a little carried away. I don't think we should get uh, that, uh close."

"OK, well I guess adrenaline can make you do things you don't mean," she said forcing a smile. "It's fine."

"No."

She blinked. His response was a lot more forceful than expected.

"I'm not saying I didn't mean it. I'm saying I have cops, ATF, and a parole officer breathing down my neck. I'm not in a position to take unnecessary risks. And you're sixteen."

"Seventeen," corrected Peri. "I'll be eighteen in April."

He paused, processing, but then shook his head. "And if this were April, we wouldn't be having this conversation, but right now, you're the definition of an unnecessary risk for me. I have to—"

She cut off whatever he was going to say next by kissing

him. For a second, she had him. His hands dug into her hair and he leaned in, and then his brain caught up.

He pushed her back into her seat. "OK, um. I don't think—you're not—"

She laughed and pulled on her gloves. Stammering Shark was adorable.

"Relax. I got it. Risk management. Keep it professional. I can handle that."

"Really? Because that did not seem like it," he said. She stepped out of the car . "I'm serious Peri. You can't just—"

She slammed the door and waved. She could see him struggling not to smile. She blew a kiss, turned, and walked away. He waited in the car until she was inside before pulling away from the curb.

Not exactly what she'd been hoping for, but at least he wasn't pretending that they hadn't had a moment. And hell, he was probably right. Keeping it professional probably was better. She could handle that. Probably.

Peregrine: Uncle Al's Craphole Apartment

Peri made phone calls and went down the to-do list required to make a Sacred Heart uniform materialize. She called for a cab to Uncle Al's and by 9:30 she was being let out in front of his apartment, but popped in at the convenience store across the street first.

"Hey Abebe," called Peri over the bonging noise as she pushed open the door.

The clerk looked up. Her hijab tonight was a festive red with a green holly-leaf print. "Hey Peri. He got home about an hour ago, but I'm kind of worried. He hasn't been in yet."

"Maybe that's a good thing," said Peri. At Abebe's doubtful look she amended, "Yeah, when is it ever good news with him? Anyway, I'm glad to see you. I got you a Christmas present."

Abebe looked shocked and delighted as Peri slid the box across the counter. "You shouldn't have!"

"I was in the city over Christmas and I saw this in a shop window. Made me think of you."

Abebe ripped open the paper. "Oh, it's lovely!" she exclaimed, lifting out a hijab in lavender with darker purple flowers. Then her eyes twinkled. "You just walked in and bought it? Did you get a few strange looks?"

Peri grinned. "Yes, but once they realized I was serious, they were extremely helpful."

Abebe came around the counter to hug her. "Thank you!"

"You're welcome! Thank you for taking care of us."

"Somebody has to," Abebe said with a smile.

Peri walked back across the street, toting her takeout boxes. Uncle Al lived on the top story of a duplex. His beat-up green Bronco was parked out front and his muddy boots were on the mat by the door, so he was definitely home. She rattled her keys loudly before opening the door. No reason to get shot.

Al was in the kitchen in his stocking feet, staring into the refrigerator. He was six-foot-ish and, true to his profession of private investigator, usually unshaven. He shared her hair color, although his was starting to have a few sprinkles of gray. "Tell me you brought food," he greeted her.

"When do I not?" she asked, hoisting the bag. "I don't know why you think your fridge is a magic food-producing box, but it really isn't."

"You pay that much for a thing, it ought to magically pro-duce something," he said, pulling bowls from the cupboard.

"I'll do that," said Peri, as she scrutinized Al's clothes. "You probably ought to go change."

Al looked at his mud-caked jeans. "Yeah, probably. Thanks." He disappeared into the bedroom and came back a few min-utes later in his faded Marine Corps sweats. He scrubbed up at the kitchen sink and sat down at the table. Peri served him his warmed-up takeout and sat down in the only other chair. Her second dinner consisted of spring rolls. Al's apartment was

Spartan in its furnishings: one couch, a coffee table, one kitchen table with two chairs, bare necessities in the kitchen, her father's flag and medals over the fireplace. Everything was scrubbed to a harsh germ-free finish and smelled faintly of Pine-Sol. Peri was used to it. She was also used to the fact that despite his OCD level of cleaning, Al never put anything away. Mail stacked up. Clothes drifted into piles along the floor. The apartment was clean, but never tidy.

He switched on the TV and watched the news. As yet, he had not poured himself a drink. Peri had to stop herself from glancing at the kitchen cabinet where he kept his booze. Abebe had said he hadn't come in after getting home, so he had to have some on hand. Unless he was on one of his periodic attempts to sober up? Those were always so painful. She would get her hopes up, and he would get frustrated or angry or something, and then he'd start drinking again, and everything would go back to the way it always was.

She got up to get a Coke and, on her way back, tried again not to eye the cupboard where he kept the Elijah Craig bourbon.

He made a derisive noise at the news and focused on his meal. The first dinner had been a lot more fun. She wondered what Al would think of Shark. Would they hate each other, or bond over a shared affinity for punching people?

"What would you think if I dated a twenty-six-year-old?" she asked.

"I think I'd have to bury another twenty-six-year-old," said Al, looking at her directly for the first time. "And aren't you still going out with that platter kid?"

Peri rolled her eyes. Al was perfectly capable of remembering Trey's name. Also, that was a terrible pun. "Yeah, I am."

"Well, then what the fuck?" His chopsticks flipped up to add the appropriate emphasis, sending a small piece of Pad Thai noodle flying.

"Trey had to move out of state to live with his cousins because his mom died." Peri specifically never mentioned Trey's uncle the drug dealer, although she had no doubt that Al had known. Al, to his credit, had never doubted that Trey wasn't cut from the same cloth. "And I have needs."

"No, you don't," said Al, digging back into his Pad Thai. "You don't have any needs until you're an adult."

"Mm. Well, you just let me know when that is," she replied.

"Who is this dipshit anyway?"

"Nobody. It doesn't matter. He doesn't want to date me anyway."

"Why? What's wrong with him?"

"Nothing's wrong with him. He just doesn't think the age difference is a good idea."

"Good. Glad he's not stupid."

Peri sighed. "Yeah. Stupider would be easier. Not as much fun, but easier."

Al gave her a distinctly exasperated look. She reached into her bag and dropped his Christmas present on the table. He pulled off the wrapping paper to reveal a box of .45 bullets.

"Thanks," he said, looking pleased.

"Hey, I know what you like."

He opened the box to inspect them. "So many shiny little friends."

"Where's your other friend—Elijah?" asked Peri.

Al rose. "Mr. Craig is staying in for the night," he said, going to the door, where his jacket was hung. From its pocket he took a small blue bag, which he tossed to her.

She caught it, feeling suspicious, and emptied the contents into her hand. Immediately she smiled. It was a thin gold necklace with a tiny charm shaped like a set of brass knuckles. "I love it!" she exclaimed, fastening it on.

"Thought you might," he said, sitting down again. "Merry Christmas."

Peri chewed her lip and decided to go for it. She'd been waiting for the right moment, and this seemed as good as any. She reached into her bag again and pulled out the pamphlet. He saw it and flung up his hands.

"Jesus, Peri, I'm not going to a support group. Three years you've been hounding me. Get it through your head. I'm not going."

"It's not for a support group," said Peri.

Al picked up the pamphlet and scanned the cover. "Dogs?"

"PTSD dogs," Peri said. "You and Dad always had dogs growing up, right?"

"No one is going to give me a dog."

"Not while you're drinking," she agreed. "But if you were on the wagon..."

"I'm pretty sure there's waiting lists and shit," he said, tossing the pamphlet down and pushing it away.

"Yeah, well, I know a guy who knows a guy. I'm just saying, if you were interested, I could probably get you a dog."

For a moment, Al looked thoughtful, and then he made a disgusted noise. "Forget about it, kid."

"Well, whatever. Can I crash here tonight?"

"Mom's at the boyfriend's place again?"

Peri nodded. She tried not to let Al know how often her mom was with Rodney. It would only complicate matters, but sometimes she didn't like to be in the house alone.

"She shouldn't stay there that much," he said disapprovingly.

"Hey, back off," said Peri. "She's entitled to a life. It took her forever to start dating after Dad died, so don't give me any horseshit about how it's inappropriate."

"That's not what I'm saying," said Al impatiently. "I'm saying maybe she shouldn't stay with him so much."

"And I'd rather she was there than bringing him home," Peri said. "We talked about it and I told her I wanted her to stay there. I mean, I didn't tell her that the idea of having some Wall Street bro loitering around the breakfast table makes me want to barf, but just that I wanted to *not* be witness to her romantic interludes."

"Not to mention that it would complicate your preferred lifestyle?" he asked sarcastically.

She looked at Al. He was in a weird-ass mood. Usually, he made his opinions of Mom and Rodney known with a well-timed eye roll. Same with her *preferred lifestyle*. In the last four years, she and Al had developed what he called *ground rules*, but there were also a few unspoken strictures. One of which was that they didn't talk about Mom. "It's a consideration," said Peri. He didn't respond and Peri relaxed enough to take a sip of her Coke.

"Does she know about the twenty-six-year-old?"

She choked on her soda. "God, no. What am I? Psychotic? She'd blow a gasket."

Al's eyebrow went up and Peri had a disturbing sense of familiarity as she recognized the expression as one she frequently wore. She wasn't used to seeing this much of herself in her uncle. From the day she'd first walked into his apartment and asked him for help, there had always been a distance between them. In one sense, it was convenient. Just like with her mother, distance made her *preferred lifestyle* possible. It was lonely, but it worked. She wasn't sure what to do with Al if he changed the rules.

The nighttime routine at Al's was simple. Watch TV until eleven, then brush teeth and go to bed, or the couch and a sleeping bag in Peri's case. It wasn't until after lights out that Peri's problems began. She went through her usual sleep routine and still found her eyelids popping open.

When she was at home, she'd usually just scarf a quarter of a pot brownie and try again. But bringing drugs, even edibles, into Uncle Al's was a bad idea. The guy had drug radar and if it wasn't bourbon then it didn't cross his doorstep. She'd tried bringing him some once after reading an article about pot being good for PTSD. He'd sent it down the garbage disposal, threw her backpack out the door, and threatened to send her on the same trajectory. It was unfortunate, really. If anyone could stand to unwind a little, it was Uncle Al.

Around two, she got up, got the scrapbook out, from under the couch and took it to the kitchen table.

She opened the pages and unfolded all the pieces of paper, laying them out. As if they could tell her something she didn't already know. Sex traffickers were taking children and selling them across the country, transporting them along the freeways like any other commodity. The most common victims were fourteen to sixteen years old, and were most often found through social media.

Peri looked at the faces of the kids that weren't here anymore. She started with Vicki, because she always started with Vicki. Then there was Sam. Then there was Patrice. Then there was Evan, Rachel, and Brittney. Sam, Patrice, and Brittney had been in foster care. Evan and Rachel came from middle-class homes. All were still enrolled in school when they'd vanished. Unlike Vicki, no bodies had ever turned up. Nobody knew where they had gone. The police said, *runaways*, like that was supposed to be the end of it.

Al had done the initial rundown on the men who had kidnapped Vicki. His notes were mostly straight from the police report. It was a small-time gang who had tried to move in on a bigger gang's territory. To Peri's relief, both the police and Al assumed that the larger gang had fought back and killed everyone at the stash house. Vicki and the other girls in the house had just been in the way.

After Vicki's body had been discovered, the case had stumbled, passed from a retiring detective to a brand new one, and then he had transferred to a different department. Nothing had moved but the paperwork from one desk to another. Periodically someone called her to re-interview her about what she remembered in the days leading up to Vicki's disappearance. They never seemed to notice that she said exactly the same thing each time. After a year and a half of nothing, Peri had decided to take matters into her own hands. Al had resisted of course, but by then she was already training at his gym, sparring men twice her size, and he was already used to her popping up with food, booze, and requests.

Before starting her investigation, Peri had assumed that most gangs were organized by neighborhood and ethnicity. And that was true, but she hadn't realized that most of those gangs fed into larger criminal organizations that operated purely for profit. It was these organizations that were pushing the large-scale trafficking.

She felt stuck.

On an individual level, she could help any one kid. That was why she'd started her business of helping people and fixing problems. She'd wanted to find the kids that needed help—the ones that didn't have anywhere else to turn and wouldn't talk to an adult. She just hadn't expected to succeed so wildly, or realized how much was boiling beneath the surface of Lincoln High School.

However, while one kid at a time was a public service, it wasn't having the dent she was hoping for. And it wasn't moving her any closer to stamping out sex trafficking in her town.

One of the reasons she'd initially approached Shark, aside from getting his help to kill Trey's scumbag drug-dealing uncle, was to see if she could pick up the scent of any trafficking in his organization. They weren't. Which was good, because had Shark been running any sort of prostitution she would have been a lot more reluctant to get in bed with him, figuratively or literally.

Which left her with the handful of clues that she'd picked up six months ago from the girls in Durrville. She got out her notes and put them down on the table.

Six months ago, she had been put in contact with Isabella. Isabella's sister Sofia had been sold by an acquaintance. Some aggressive questioning of the acquaintance had led to another middleman who had provided a phone number. Using the phone number and the help of Cerise, a local hacker, Peri had traced the location of the phone to Durrville. They'd gone to the location only to realize that Sofia and two other girls were being moved as they watched. Peri had chosen to rescue the girls rather than follow the thread further up the food chain.

What little Sofia and the girls had remembered was that they had all been exchanged from one buyer to another at a location on the freeway, under an overpass, near Peri's hometown. It had taken Peri six months to figure out which overpass. She saw why it was preferred. It was a traffic camera dead zone, in an industrial area, and out of view of passing cars. It was ideal for illegal exchanges. But to date, her efforts to get surveillance on the overpass had netted her absolutely nothing.

Al came out of the bedroom and she pushed her notes under some of the other papers. Al would not approve of the Durrville incident.

"Stop looking at that thing," he said, going to the sink for a glass of water.

"I have accomplished exactly zero of my high school goals," said Peri bitterly.

"I thought you managed to ace all those AP classes or whatever. And aren't you getting college credit with that Running Start thing?"

Peri was startled. She hadn't thought Al had been paying attention when she talked about her school plans. "I'm talking about real world goals," she said. "Not my grade point average."

"Yeah," he said. She waited, but nothing else seemed to be forthcoming. Apparently, paying attention to the fact that she took AP classes and Running Start was as far as she could expect him to go. Which was nice, but it didn't do her much good. She gave an exasperated sigh and tucked the papers back into the album.

"Don't give me that shit," said Al. "Most kid's high school goals don't include taking down criminal organizations. I'm not equipped to respond to this kind of existential crisis at 3:00 A.M."

"Is there a time when you are equipped for it? Because I could come back then."

He seemed to think about it. "No," he said after a moment. "I'm barely coping with having a teenage girl around. I don't understand why Chris couldn't have had a boy."

Since he said this at least once a month, it only made Peri smile. "Go back to bed, Uncle Al."

He pointed at the couch. "*You* go back to bed."

Peri tucked the book away and climbed into her sleeping bag. He waited until she was in before turning off the lights.

"It's not down to you, you know," he said in the dark. "It's not your job. The police and the Feds do have people working on it."

"Yeah, I know," said Peri. "But they don't care like I do."

Four Years Ago

Peri & Al

Thirteen-year-old Peri knocked on the door. He didn't answer. She tried the handle and it opened easily—not locked. She walked through the apartment. It smelled clean, but it looked like a shithole. Did he never put anything away? There was a giant pile of mail on the coffee table—like he just brought the mail in from the box and dropped it there.

Early afternoon sunshine streamed through the spotless front window. She was supposed to be in Algebra class right now. It was the first time she'd ever skipped on purpose. She supposed that should seem exciting. It didn't feel exciting. It felt like Algebra was inconvenient. Most of school felt that way these days.

Her dad's flag was over the fireplace and she found that she was avoiding looking at it. Irritated at herself, she edged closer and stared at the picture of her father tucked into the box beside the medals. She didn't really see a resemblance.

There was a snort from one of the bedrooms and she tiptoed over to the open doorway, hoping like hell he was alone. He was. He was also fully clothed and face down in the pillows.

"Uncle Al!"

He didn't move. She went closer to the bed. She could see him breathing, so at least he wasn't dead. She yelled his name a few more times, with no reaction. Eventually, she kicked the bed frame.

Al popped upright in the bed like he was on springs and pointed a gun at her. She waited, arms crossed, for him to recognize her.

"Jesus, kid." He swung his legs over the side of the bed and rubbed his face. "Ever hear of knocking?"

"I knocked, I yelled. You didn't answer."

"What do you want?"

"I need to know how to kill someone."

He turned to her, his face angry and alien. "You take a gun, put it against their head." He put the gun barrel against her temple. "And then you pull the trigger."

"Yeah," she said, staring into his red-rimmed eyes. "I got that far. What do I do when I don't have a gun?"

They stayed that way for a long moment, neither backing down nor blinking. Eventually, he put the gun down on the pillow and rubbed his face again. "Then you get a gun," he said tiredly.

"I can't carry a gun, Uncle Al. What am I supposed to do at school—leave it in my locker? They get checked. I need something I can carry on me at all times. Is a Taser any good? It doesn't seem like it would be."

"No, they suck. More than one assailant and you're screwed. You'd want a knife, I guess. No, what am I saying. You don't want anything. Why do you want to kill someone?"

She hesitated, debating how much to tell him. "I don't want to kill anyone right this minute. But last week my friend Vicki was kidnapped. Do you remember her? You met her at my birthday party."

"I don't remember your birthday, so no, I don't remember her."

"That's OK, in a month no one else will remember her either. No one at school but Trey really gives a shit about her. But anyway, she was kidnapped."

He stared at her. "What do you mean kidnapped?"

"I mean that she went to buy weed from a guy and he picked her up and put her in his van. Then he drove her two towns over and gave her to some sex traffickers. You know what happens to girls after that?"

He didn't reply, seeming to concentrate on untying his boot laces.

"They shoot you up, then they brand you, then they rape you, you know, so you get used to it. Then they sell you to as many men as they want."

"That's not going to happen to you," he said roughly. "You don't have to worry about that."

"Really? Why not? Is my dad going to walk me to school every day? Oh, wait, yeah, he can't, he's dead."

He threw one of his boots across the room where it hit the wall with an impressive bang and left a mark.

"I meant," he said through gritted teeth, "she must have been hanging with the wrong people. She should have—"

"She should have what? Not bought weed? Did she deserve that for buying weed?"

"No, that's not what I'm saying. I just mean, she shouldn't have..."

"Gone to the mall?"

He went into the kitchen, forcing Peri to follow him. "I'm sure she'd tell you that she knew something was off about that guy. She should have listened to her instincts." He rummaged in the cupboard until he found an empty glass.

"Well, she might tell me that, except that a rival gang broke in and shot everyone in the house, including Vicki. So, she's not telling anyone anything, you know, ever again."

He paused, bottle hovering above the glass. "You'll want something light weight, folding, single-edged, easy to open."

"Great, can I get that at the Sportco? Or do I have to order online? Is there a best brand?"

"The police will take care of it. Why are you doing this?"

"Doing what? Giving a shit? Wanting to protect myself? Is there something wrong with that?" Even Peri could hear the edge of hysteria in her voice. She tamped it back down. He wouldn't do what she wanted if she got emotional. Al couldn't handle emotions. "I want to know how to stop this from happening to me," she said more calmly.

"Peri," he sighed.

"Just tell me what I need to know and you can go back to hating yourself or whatever."

He emptied the bottle into the glass, but it was barely half full. "How about you just go buy me more bourbon," he replied, slamming the bottle down on the counter.

"I'm thirteen, Uncle Al. How am I supposed to buy bourbon?"

"If you're old enough to kill someone, you're old enough to buy booze. There's a convenience store across the street. Go make it happen."

They stared at each other.

"Fine." She marched out of the house, down the stairs. She crossed the street and pushed open the door to the convenience store with a bang. A Muslim woman in a headdress was watching her from behind the register.

"Hi," she said. "Do you know my Uncle Al? Lives across the street? Buys bourbon?"

"Yes," the cashier admitted.

Peri dug in her pocket. "He's agreed to shower and clean his apartment if I buy booze. This is the cash I have." She dropped three fifties on the counter. "Can you help me out with that?"

The cashier marked one of the fifties with the special pen that indicated if it was counterfeit. The color remained bright yellow. "Yes," she agreed, after a long moment of indecision.

"Great. Which one is bourbon?"

The cashier pointed at the shelf. "He likes the Elijah Craig."

"Fine." Peri reached for the biggest bottle.

"But…"

"But what?"

"Well…" More hesitation. "He's an alcoholic, OK?"

"I had noticed."

"If you buy the big bottle, he'll just drink the big bottle. If you get smaller bottles, you can probably get him to ration it, you know?"

"Thank you! That is a great tip!" Peri gathered up three of the smaller bottles and then, after a moment's thought, a fourth. "I want him to clean out the refrigerator too," she said to the cashier's questioning look. "Keep the change," she added, realizing that this might not be the only time she had to bribe her. Might as well get her in the habit.

Back upstairs in Al's apartment, she pulled a bottle out of the bag and put it on the table.

"You couldn't get anything bigger?"

"I have three more in the bag," she said. "But I'm also going to have to know how to use a knife once I have one."

Al sighed, his head hanging down. "This is a bad idea."

Tuesday ~ December 27

Shark: The Warehouse

Geier officially held one meeting per month with all the territory bosses. There were other meetings throughout the month, but at the end of it everyone was in the same place at the same time. As usual, the meeting was in the warehouse that held staging furniture for his various real-estate sales.

Today the floor was set with swoopy chaise lounges and Grecian columns. It looked like a video shoot for an eighties rock ballad. Shark half-expected a fog machine to start spewing out clouds and a girl in a flowing dress and big hair to run through. The chaise lounges looked like Annibale Colombo knock-offs. They didn't quite have the Italian firm's flare, but were probably a quarter of the price. However, he was certain that Geier was selling them at the high-end number.

Shark watched the room fill in and worked to maintain a straight face as grown men tried to figure out how to sit on a chaise lounge and look tough. Shark moved his, making an annoying squealing noise as he rotated it to point the foot at Geier. Then sat down and lounged back, feet up, with his drink and shades, pretending he was at the beach. Marko took up position behind him. Several other men gave him dirty looks, probably because they wished they'd thought of it.

This meeting was all about Crease, who had opted to sit in the middle of his lounger and face Geier with no back support. Like Shark, he was recently out of prison and looking to show his usefulness. Unlike Shark, Geier had simply welcomed him back in. No hoops to jump through—just *welcome back Crease*.

What worried Shark was that he didn't know why. Crease was a black guy a few years older than Shark, named for the scar that ran along his left temple where a bullet had creased his skull. They had about the same body count. Similar background. What was it? Why was Shark on the outside and Crease in? Simply a matter of timing? Did Geier know something?

The main topic was the leak in the supply line. Crease laid out the actions he'd taken so far. Shark was glad to hear he'd made practically no progress. Crease had started at packaging and was working his way down the distribution lines looking for leaks. It was a thankless task guaranteed to ruffle the feathers of anyone he turned his attention to.

The other territory bosses were weighing in with opinions and he could tell they were all making Geier impatient. Geier's long fingers were tapping in a repetitive waterfall of movement on the arm of his chair.

"Shark!" Geier snapped. Shark knew what Geier wanted was for Shark to sit up, jump to attention, be a good boy, so instead he took a sip of his drink and didn't move from his reclined position. "You've been remarkably quiet. Perhaps you would care to share your opinion."

"I would not," said Shark, which silenced the room. Now they were all staring at him, but he wasn't about to hand Crease the solution. "Jerome is handling it. He doesn't need me to tell him how to do his job."

Crease turned his attention to Shark, his lips thinning as they compressed into a straight line of annoyance. Shark smiled pleasantly, knowing that using his real name would bug the shit out of Crease. Shark had every intention of staying out of the guy's way—he just didn't see why he had to play nice while he did it.

"Well, what if I want to know what you would do?" asked Geier, forcing the issue. Geier could never stop himself from picking and tearing at everyone, even if it didn't necessarily benefit him, and today his talons were definitely out.

"I thought you didn't like it when I made other people's problems, my problems," said Shark and instantly regretted it.

Geier's hard brown eyes narrowed, but his smile widened. "Well, Jerome's not exactly Stanley, now, is he?"

Shark knew that meant nothing to anyone else in the room. No one remembered Stanley and Shark had no intention of enlightening them. He also had no intention of battling Geier today. He stood up and went over to the drink cart, dropping a few more ice cubes into his glass while he carefully picked his next words. "We need to know where the leak is, but right now we're being pushed by the Scarecrows. We need to push back. I guess you could roll up on a couple of his guys. Find out who they're getting the product from. Chase it up their food chain instead of down ours. Either way the job gets done."

A vein was throbbing in Crease's temple. "Any other suggestions?" he asked, through clenched teeth.

Geier smiled as he took a sip from his glass. Crease's anger made him happy.

"No," said Shark, going back to his chaise and returning to his former position. "I've got my own problems. I don't have time to think about yours."

"Right," growled Crease. "The ATF Agent. You haven't handled him yet? How hard is it to put down one man?"

Shark heard Marko snort in irritation. "Depends on your goals." Shark shrugged, refusing to take it personally.

"When will you have it handled?" asked Geier. "I don't want this to interfere with business. As you have pointed out, your territory is only recently in the black. I'd hate to see backsliding."

"Soon," said Shark.

"That's vague," Crease said.

"Ask Cassius how much I like discussing my plans in public," said Shark.

Geier laughed and the rest of the room shifted uncomfortably. Cassius was the last person who had delved too deeply into Shark's plans and he was no longer around to discuss what he'd discovered. "Fine, play it your way. But I am assuming that you do have plans in place?"

Shark nodded.

"Good. Then I will expect to see results before next month's meeting."

"Not a problem." Shark said, hoping he wasn't lying.

He exited the building with Marko, and as usual Shark

forced his stride to be slow and methodical, quelling the urge to get away as quickly as possible.

"Well, that sucked monkey tits," said Marko once they were in the car.

Shark added *monkey tits* to his Marko lexicon. "Definitely."

"I wish the meeting could have happened after we hit Fowler's computer. I hate having absolutely nothing. What are we going to do if the laptop doesn't get us anything?" asked Marko.

"It will get us something."

Marko looked worried.

"I'll come up with something," Shark promised.

Eleven Years Ago

15

Shark & Stanley

Fifteen-year-old Shark sauntered out of the convenience store, a beer in each pants leg and a *Playboy* in his waistband. He rounded the corner and pulled out the contraband. Everything was drooping and sticky in the summer heat. Opening a beer, he headed toward the condemned house where he and Stanley were crashing. The junkies who flopped there with them were still nodding out—they wouldn't move until after dark. They all smelled because there was no running water, so he didn't like to go inside while they were around. Shark hit a youth shelter every few days for a shower, but it was a risk because the cops were looking for him.

He was sitting on the front porch reading a classic reprint article called *Sex is Politics*. He wasn't sure he totally got what the guy was saying, but a lot of it sounded like the shit that Geier spouted.

There was some stuff about Greeks and gays and women, but what it boiled down to was politicians using religious morality to control the population. He went back up and reread a paragraph. He had the feeling he was missing out on a lot of the references. He was going have to go look shit up in the dictionary at the library.

Stanley jogged around the corner and Shark automatically flipped to the centerfold, so he wouldn't be caught reading.

Stanley had a fresh black eye and a split lip. Shark scrutinized the injuries critically. Stanley was also fifteen. Like Shark he was half-Puerto Rican, but Stanley's dad had been black. Because of that, both he and Stanley had both been ostracized from the neighborhood gangs. Geier was the only one who would take them.

"What'd you do?" asked Shark. "Try and hold out on Devo again?" Stanley was always trying to short the payments to their supplier. Shark didn't blame him exactly—Shark liked money and eating too—but Stanley was no good at disguising his crimes.

Stanley shook his head. "Geier."

Shark sighed. Geier had a temper and Stanley always seemed to push his buttons. "I keep telling you to keep your mouth shut."

"I didn't even say anything this time," protested Stanley.

Shark found that unlikely. "OK, then what'd you do?"

"I didn't do anything! I don't know why you always take his side."

"I don't take his side. I just know you." Shark had tried to explain to Stanley that his great ideas and shortcuts were never as subtle or clever as Stanley thought they were. Geier would only let them get away with shortcuts that cut him in on the action. Geier was the beast that had to be fed.

Stanley shifted from foot to foot. Shark had a bad feeling.

"I may have mentioned that big score that we took down last week to Virgil."

Shark groaned. "Stan! What the hell, man? You're lucky Geier didn't shoot you."

"What's the big deal? I was shooting craps with some guys from around the block and it came up. They thought it was cool. It's not that big of a deal. Only then that fucker Jorge ratted me out to Geier. I don't see why it's a problem."

Shark looked for a way to explain the circle of life to Stanley. "OK, you know how we buy our product from Devo and then we cut it and sell it? Well, Devo does the same thing from Geier. And Geier does the same thing from Achey."

"So what?"

"And you know how if Devo finds out that we upped our rates and are making more money, suddenly his prices go up?"

"Yeah," said Stanley sourly.

"OK, well, what do you think is going to happen if Achey finds out Geier is making more money?" Stanley's face showed consternation. "Basically, you just cost Geier a shit-ton of paper because you couldn't keep your mouth shut."

"Oh fuck," groaned Stanley. "What am I going to do?"

"Well, what did Geier say when Jorge told him?"

Now Stanley looked nervous. "He just punched me twice and ran off. I didn't stick around to see if he was coming back."

Shark ran his hand through his hair. "OK, you stay here. I'll go up to the house and nose around. See what's the burn."

"And what if it's burning in the direction of killing Stanley?"

"If he was going to kill you, he would have just done it,"

Shark assured him, mentally crossing his fingers. "Don't worry. Let me find out what's up before we panic."

"Yeah, but what are you going to do?"

"I don't know yet, but I'll think of something."

"Cool," said Stanley, dropping down onto the porch and opening the other beer. "What?" he said in response to Shark's expression. "You said you were going up to the house. It's not like you were going to drink it before it got warm. I'll go steal you another one when you get back."

Shark folded the *Playboy*, put it in his back pocket, and walked the half-mile to the subway station. He had to wait until the station guard was looking somewhere else before hopping the turnstile. Geier lived in a house seven stops uptown. It was a few miles and an entire world away. Geier's house was on the edge of a neighborhood on the point of gentrification. The neighborhood, a mix of commercial buildings and dilapidated duplexes, was slowly being renovated out of recognition. Old warehouses were now lofts and the houses soon wouldn't be affordable to the people that Shark thought of as normal. It was Shark's guess that it wouldn't be too long before the street-level kids were warned to stay away from the house. He'd heard rumors that Geier was looking for other locations for the gang to meet at, but he hadn't seen any actual progress on that front.

Shark went around to the back, because he knew where he was in the pecking order. Jorge was at the back door.

"Shark, I don't know if you want to come in here," Jorge warned him. "Your boy Stanley has pissed off the man, but good."

"I heard. How bad is it?"

"Shit's been bad between him and Achey for a couple of months. This might put the whole thing in the crapper."

Shark frowned. "Did Geier go to talk to Achey?"

"Yeah," Jorge said, "But it must not have gone great, because he's back already. You really want to go in?"

Shark squinted across the gravel parking strip and tried to guess the future. "Yeah, I think I do."

"What are you going to say?"

"I'll think of something."

Jorge looked unimpressed. Shark went up the back stairs to Geier's study, trying to map out a strategy. If the world were perfect, Geier would take over from Achey. Achey was always screwing shit up for the crews. Geier ran a tight ship, and Achey used him to compensate for the messes of the less organized. If Geier took over then they wouldn't have to deal with that shit. But how could Geier do that? Guys disappeared all the time. Maybe someone could whack Achey? It would be tough to get a shot at him. A steroid fiend and gym rat, Achey usually rolled with a full crew.

A memory sparked and in the dim light of the upstairs hallway, Shark smiled.

He went into the study and waited for Geier to acknowledge him. Fuzz and the other leg-breakers were discussing the week's non-payers and what strategies would be utilized to make them cough up the dough.

Geier kept the window covered with heavy curtains ever since the time that someone had taken a pot-shot at him from the building across the street, so the room was always dark, even in the summer, and smelled faintly of meat, because Geier always ate steak for lunch. Shark couldn't remember the last time he'd had actual meat. Mostly for proteins he subsisted on cans of refried beans, cheese, and the disgusting sticks of jerky that Stanley always pinched.

Geier sat behind an expensive wood desk. He appeared focused on Fuzz and the others, but one hand began to drum the desk—his long fingers rising and falling in the steady rhythm of anger.

Eventually the crew filed out and only Fuzz and Geier remained. Geier got up to pour himself a drink. "You here to do the right thing and tell me where Stanley is?"

"No," said Shark. "I came to ask how we can fix the problem."

"You're making Stanley's problems your problems?" asked Geier.

"Stanley's a good guy. He just gets carried away."

"I don't give a shit if he's Mother fucking Theresa," said Geier. "He fucked me over. Now Achey's holding my feet to the fire because Stanley can't keep his mouth shut."

"I've been thinking about that," said Shark. "And wouldn't it be…" He hesitated. Geier had always encouraged him to think strategically, but this was the first time he'd ever applied the principles to Geier's business. If Geier took offense, it wouldn't just be Stanley's head on the chopping block. "Wouldn't it be better for us if Achey wasn't around?"

Geier stared at him.

"Kid thinks he's big time," rumbled Fuzz. Shark ignored

him. He didn't like the square headed leg breaker with his hedge-
hog haircut—Fuzz enjoyed hurting people who couldn't fight
back.

Geier sipped his drink. "Sure. It would be real fucking great.
You got a plan on how to make that happen?"

"On Tuesdays and Thursdays, he does cardio with a trainer
named Marigold," said Shark.

"Trainer?" repeated Fuzz skeptically.

Shark shrugged. "He goes at five in the morning, by himself."

"And you know this how?" asked Geier.

"Same way that Achey knows about last week's score. Stanley
talks to people and people talk to Stanley. That's why he's good
at sales."

Geier continued to stare at Shark. Shark tried to stare back,
but found himself blinking. "Fuzz," Geier said, "tomorrow
morning, I want you take Stanley and my little problem-solver
here and see if there's any truth to what they're saying."

"Be here tomorrow at four," said Fuzz.

Stanley was asleep on the porch when he returned.

"Stan!" He kicked Stan's foot and Stan popped up, reaching
for the gun in his waistband.

"What's the word?" asked Stan, sitting down again.

"Jerkass Tim, that kid from juvie. His story about Achey and
the trainer named Marigold. That was true, right?"

"Far as I know," said Stanley. "Why?"

"Because our lives depend on it," said Shark.

Stanley rubbed sleep from his eyes. "I'm sure it will work
out."

"Based on what?" demanded Shark.

"You always get us through," Stanley said.

Shark nodded, but privately he wondered how long he could keep doing it. Someday, his luck was going to run out—and one or both of them would have to pay up.

Tuesday ~ December 27

Peregrine: Town Center Shopping Mall

As she made her way across the plaza, Peri adjusted her bags and checked her phone, frowning at her mother's email. She was vaguely aware that the maintenance worker who was holding the ladder for the guy removing holiday decorations from the light poles was watching her ass. She thought about flipping him off, but decided to ignore it. She could only fight so many battles in one day. She mentally checked off the items on her mother's shopping list. What the fuck was wrong with old people? Why on earth would anyone want half this shit? Her phone vibrated and a message popped up.

THE CALL IS COMING FROM INSIDE THE HOUSE.

Below it was a picture of herself from a moment ago.

Her head snapped up. Shark was sitting at one of the outdoor tables. He waved, but with a slightly pained expression. He looked as if it had just now occurred to him that taking stalker photos might not be a good idea. She burst out laughing. Embarrassed Shark was almost as good as stammering Shark.

She plunked her bags down on his table. "Aw, my first stalker. I'm sure that will end well for everyone."

"I'll be in a shallow grave by the end of the week, won't I?"

"You'll be lucky to make it that long. Did you need me for something? You could just text, you know. Stalking is so 2002."

"Actually, I was looking for a decent coffee and there you were. Which sort of makes up for the coffee."

"Yeah, their coffee is meh, at best," she said. She perched on the edge of the table, her feet on the other chair, leaning forward slightly to put her arms around her knees.

"What are you doing here?" he asked. "It's a bit late for Christmas shopping."

"Mom's work holiday party is always after the twenty-fifth, and as usual she didn't have time to shop." Her mother's work as an event planner almost invariably meant that she was slammed through the holiday season. "So I'm helping." She wished she'd said something cooler. *I'm helping* sounded like she was twelve. "I got almost everything on her list, but I'm stuck on this." She held out her phone to show him the third entry on the email list: CORN STRIPPER.

"I don't think that's an appropriate thing to send your daughter to purchase," he said in a snooty, disapproving tone that was so unlike him that she laughed. He grinned, but promptly took out his phone and Googled it.

She craned to look at the results with him. "So, you take corn off a cob with it? Why would anyone want that? Well, I guess I could try the kitchen store. Seriously, what nutjob doesn't just use a knife?"

"Perhaps not everyone is as knife-centric as you?" he suggested.

Peri chuckled. "Possibly not, but I don't think that justifies the existence of a corn stripper." She tilted her head at him thoughtfully. He'd said they had to keep things professional, but that was a no to making out, not to *hanging* out, right? She liked talking to him. Couldn't they just be friends? He grimaced as he took another sip of his beverage. "If you walk with me, I'll show you where to buy real coffee."

He hesitated for a fraction of a second. "Sold," he said, arcing his cup into the garbage can.

They wove through the crowded square and out onto an open walkway between the stores.

"So, tell me," she said, "Are you a mocha person or latte person?"

"I'm a coffee with a little cream and sugar person," he said. "I like my coffee to taste like coffee and my chocolate to taste like chocolate. Why people insist on blending them into some sort of mutant monster, I will never know."

"But tell me how you really feel," she said, and slipped on a patch of ice.

Her feet went out from under her and there was a second of freefall and then Shark grabbed her around the waist. Her bags whacked him as she flailed, trying to find her balance, which would have been easier if she'd been able to stop laughing. Finally, breathless and clutching his coat, she managed to find a precarious stability.

"I never thought I'd die on a patch of ice," she said, staring up at him. God, did he have to be so gorgeous? And did she have to be wearing so many layers? This would be a lot more fun if she could just snuggle up against his chest. So much for being just friends. She did not feel friendly right now.

"Don't even think about it," he said. "Otherwise I'm stuck with Domingo in a dress for tomorrow."

How did he always manage to keep such a straight face? There was only the tiniest hint of laughter in his eyes. She wanted to make him smile for real.

"That's it. You're going out with me," she said, tugging threateningly at his coat.

"I think not." He tightened his grip and lifted her off the ice and onto his slushy, but stable, section of sidewalk.

A smattering of applause from a group of power-walking grandmas in winter workout gear brought Peri back to an awareness that they weren't alone.

"Nice save," one yelled. Shark acknowledged the praise with a wave. He looked back down at her and Peri found herself blushing and half-burying her face in his coat.

"Don't like being the center of attention?" He was smiling for real this time, but it was a soft smile, free of laughter.

"Not when I'm being me," said Peri, trying to regain some of her dignity.

"Kitchen store is this way?" He inclined his head to the left, still smiling down at her. She nodded, smiling back. He kept his arm around her all the way to the store.

They stomped off their boots as they entered, shedding slush and chunks of salt and ice. Now Shark wore an expression of pained skepticism.

"Not a fan of the kitchen store?" she asked, trying to see it from his point of view.

"Everything is so..." He paused. "Everything here is an accessory."

She tried to parse the meaning of that. What did accessories mean to someone like Shark? Extra? Meaningless? Useless? She took in the shelves of gadgets and tools. He was right. He was the kind of person who was probably used to dealing in necessities. That seemed... sad? Shouldn't he have extras?

She picked up what looked like a small silicone doll of an angry woman with hands on her hips.

"Hi Shark," she said, holding it up in front of her face, and giving it a goofy voice, "I'm the world's worst and tiniest sex doll!" He choked on a laugh. "Seriously," she said, putting it down, "what is this?"

"Well, obviously it's a..." he checked the tag, "hot mama microwave cleaner. What else could it possibly be?"

"Oh, obviously. I can't believe I didn't see it earlier. What about this one?" She held up something that looked like a miniature tripod.

"It's for massaging potatoes."

She giggled and reached for the next thing she saw—a metal-handled implement with multiple prongs—for his assessment.

"Moustache pick. No, actually," he said, looking at it more closely, "I know that one. It's for holding down vegetables while you cut them. Marko has one, but he says it's only good for stabbing people."

She gave it an experimental swipe. "I could see that."

"Serial killer," he whispered in her ear, and she poked him with the tool.

"Take that back!"

He grinned and shook his head.

"Can I help you?" asked a sales clerk. He was eyeing Peri's handling of the vegetable tool with disfavor.

"Yes," said Peri. "We just moved in together and we don't have hardly anything we need in the kitchen. We are desperate, just desperate, for a corn stripper."

"Aisle four," said the sales clerk suspiciously.

"And a French press," Shark said.

"Of course." The clerk led the way further into the store.

Thirty minutes later, they left with the corn stripper, a French press, and a knife sharpener. And Shark had smiled at her at least eight times.

17

Shark: Leo's Pawn Shop

"I'll pay you back when we get in the car and I can find whatever bag I've dumped my wallet into," Peri said as they waited for his coffee.

"Why?"

"Because you just bought a knife sharpener for me and a corn stripper for my mother."

He'd never had a girl offer to pay him back for anything before. It was a novel concept. Also, he was pretty sure the look of satisfaction on her face had been well worth the money. Shark had dropped Marko off at the bowling alley and cruised back toward his condo, but not wanting to return home, he'd pulled in at the local shopping mall and looked for a coffee shop. He'd been hoping that maybe he could caffeinate his brain into coming up with something brilliant. Instead, he'd seen Peri coming across the plaza and promptly forgotten everything else.

"Don't bother," he said.

"No, I shouldn't let you do that. I'll pay you back."

He thought it over some more. "No," he said, and she laughed.

"You can't just veto."

"Sure I can." Her bottom lip started to pucker in a frown.

"Relax. Call it a Christmas gift or a bonus for doing the Sacred Heart thing on such short notice."

"Mm," she said, but didn't argue further.

Coffee achieved, Shark ushered Peri into his car. Around them the Valentine's Day pink and red was already starting to replace the wreaths and bells. The mall was yet another reminder that he wasn't in the city. In the city, stores seemed to evolve like parasites or mold, clustering together as they cannibalized and spread. Here the mall looked like it was trying to build a theme park version of the city with cheerful touches of forced character and flair. The concrete was too clean. The garbage was *in* the cans. Even the snow looked cleaner. He didn't like it.

Peri turned on the radio and they fell into a companionable silence as she checked her phone. He'd hooked up with girls who managed to make sex boring, but he'd never met one who could make a kitchen store entertaining.

Her phone rang and he saw Trey's face pop up. He felt a stab of jealousy. He'd noticed she was wearing a new necklace—gold with a tiny set of brass knuckles. It was exactly the kind of thing he would have picked out for her, but considering that she usually didn't wear jewelry unless she was working, he had to wonder where it had come from. Maybe Trey was a better boyfriend than Shark guessed? He was developing a strong desire to punch Trey.

"Hey Trey," she said, picking up without hesitation. He could hear Trey talking, but not what he said. "No," she replied, "I'm on my way home from picking up stuff for my mom. Yeah, I got a ride with a friend."

Yeah, sure. He was a friend. He was a friend giving a friend a ride home. In a friendly way. Like friends do.

There was more talking from Trey. "Oh. Hm. I don't know the answer to that one. I can probably dig it up once I get back home." Trey said something that made her laugh. "Sounds good. I'll ping you once I'm at home. OK, bye!"

"Research booty call?" asked Shark.

"Heh. Sort of. We did a group paper last year, and he wants some of the research we did for it. Oh! Is that Leo's Pawn Shop?"

It was indeed. Leo was definitely on Marko's list of people who owed money to the Fives. They'd booked him for an in person visit next week. Not that Leo was aware of that.

She put her hand on his leg. "Do you mind if we stop?"

He gave her a disbelieving look.

"You don't have to come in. I've got this thing. Long story. But basically, something I need got pawned and I've been checking all the shops. This one was next on my list."

Shark thought that sounded like a load of crap. "Sure, why not?"

While Peri went inside, he texted Marko. Marko shot back a photo of Leo and a status of his account. Shark checked his watch. Peri was taking too long.

He went around the back of the shop and knocked on the back door. It opened a crack. "Marko sent me," Shark said quietly.

The door opened further and a knuckle-dragger with a bald head peered out. "We're paid up through the end of the month," he complained.

Shark grabbed the handle and slammed the door open into

the man's face, following it with a punch to the gut and a kick to the knee. There was a satisfying crunch and the knuckle dragger went down, groaning.

"Stay down if you know what's good for you," said Shark and stepped over him. He walked through the back room and out to the front where Leo appeared to be saying something suggestive to Peri.

"I wouldn't recommend it," replied Peri, which was a sure sign that Leo was about to encounter something bad in his life. Although, in this instance, it turned out to be Shark's fist.

"Shark!" she exclaimed.

"Oh shit," muttered Leo through his bleeding nose. Shark pulled the gun out from under the counter and out of Leo's reach.

"You can't just punch everyone who's rude to me," said Peri.

"Why not?"

That seemed to stymie her. "Well, because for one thing, I periodically like to punch my own people."

"Little bird, the last time I let you punch your own people I had to send Marko out for tarps." He pressed the release button on the lock and she stepped into the pawn shop's cage.

"That is…" she hesitated.

"Completely true?"

"Not the point," she said, her eyes twinkling, as she pretended to pout.

"Well, then let's just say that I like you to save your hands for other things," he said. "Now can we get whatever it is you wanted and go?"

"Go? But don't you want to meet Leo? I'm sure you'd like to hear some of the other things he was saying before you came in."

She snuggled against him, leaning up to his face, and he found himself hoping that she'd get carried away and kiss him. But at the last moment, she turned back to Leo. "Leo, have you met Shark? This is Shark."

Leo waved weakly. "I wasn't really serious before. I was just joking."

"Really?" Peri mocked a confused frown. "I could swear you were serious about me blowing your chubby meat popsicle."

Leo choked and made a high-pitched wheezing noise. "No, definitely not. I was just joking. Definitely joking. What can I uh… do for you?"

"Give her what she wants," Shark said.

Peri smiled sweetly. "Please," she added, and Leo gulped like it was the scariest word he'd ever heard.

"Yeah, of course," he said, edging past Shark. "It was this one?" He reached for a video camera and handed it to her, shifting nervously from foot to foot as Peri popped open the back and inspected the contents.

"Where's the memory card?"

"I took it out," said Leo.

"Tell me you didn't wipe it," she said.

"No, I never do shit with them. I just put them in the bin." He produced a Tupperware container from under the counter. It was filled with memory cards of all kinds.

"You can't cut him," said Shark, reading Peri's expression.

"Not even a little? I mean, like, maybe just take an ear off?"

Leo clapped a hand over his ears.

"No. Marko has to look at him. Marko has a thing about ears."

Peri rolled her eyes. "I cannot catch a break."

"Just take them all," said Shark. "You can look through them later."

"Fine." Peri dumped the camera in with the memory cards and took the container out of Leo's unresisting hands. "How much do I owe you?"

"Yes, Leo," said Shark, smiling with all of his teeth. "How much does she owe you?"

Leo looked from Shark to Peri and back. "Uh, consider it a gift. Yeah, a gift."

"Good choice, Leo," said Shark. "Another good choice would be to pay Marko next time he comes for a visit." Leo blanched.

Shark escorted Peri out to the car, opening the doors for her as she went. She did her part by adding extra sway to her walk.

"Oh my God!" she exclaimed, as they pulled out onto the roadway. "You are so much fun!"

He wasn't sure what reaction he'd been expecting, but that hadn't been it. He took his eyes off the road to look at her. Her eyes sparkled and she was kneeling in the passenger seat. She was all kinds of unsafe.

"I might actually consider co-workers if I could have someone like you. I'm serious. I hardly ever take anyone with me on these things because everyone gets all weird the second I bring up something like ears."

"Stick with me," he said. "We can rip off all the best pawn shops together. Or at least all the ones that are making book through Marko."

"I bet we could take all the other ones too."

He found himself considering that prospect as she leaned toward him.

"I am taking you home before you talk me into embarking on a three-state crime spree," he said, forcing his gaze back to the road. "Aren't you supposed to be one of the good guys? All helping people and shit?"

She leaned over to whisper in his ear, "I'm not that good." Her breath on his ear was like an electric jolt along his entire nervous system. He instinctively turned back to her again. The way she was biting her lip made him want to pull over. He wasn't sure what she saw in his face, but she collapsed back into the passenger seat, laughing. "It's too bad you want to keep things so professional," she said, looking out the window. "You're hot when you're working."

Wednesday ~ December 28

Shark: The Condo

Shark woke up to a pair of tits in his face. Vivian had crashed with him again, and she liked morning sex. Another reason they were wildly incompatible. He hated mornings and he hated dealing with another human being before coffee. It also didn't help that last night she'd left a set of claw marks down his back that still stung. Sex with Vivian required jujitsu skills and a safe word, and while that might be occasionally entertaining it wasn't his idea of a relaxing time. This morning, he flipped her over so he wouldn't have to look her in the face. When they were done, he pulled on some clothes, stole a cigarette from her purse, and went out on the bedroom balcony.

He watched the gray water of the pond and pondered the asshole tromping along that path at the edge. Who did that? It was cold and snowy. Just stay indoors and get a fucking treadmill. As he watched, the man stopped to take a picture of birds. Fucking nature enthusiasts should die.

His phone rang. "Hey Marko."

"Hey, I'm in your parking lot, and it looks like your overly-friendly PO is still up there?"

"Yeah, give me about twenty minutes to get rid of her."

"No problem," said Marko. "I'm going to get a coffee. You want anything?"

"Just get me a black coffee," said Shark, knowing that Marko would still come back with something weird. So far, their working relationship was perfect except for Marko's complete lack of understanding about what constituted coffee. Vivian came out of the bedroom dressed in his shirt and her socks.

"It's your apartment," she said, putting her arms around him. "You could smoke inside."

"I don't like the place smelling like cigarettes," he said, not adding that she smelled like cigarettes.

"You're such a hypocrite." She took the cigarette from his mouth and finished it with a long drag.

"I thought that was the basis of our relationship," he said. "Speaking of which, you can't spend the night anymore. Marko and the guys are starting to drop by more. They can't see you here."

"Oh, you don't know, your stock might go up if they found out you were nailing your parole officer."

"Or they might start to wonder why I'm spending so much time with law enforcement."

"I think you underestimate how hot I am," she smirked. Disentangling herself from him, she stubbed out the cigarette.

"You overestimate how much I care," said Shark. "You should try remembering that the entire goal is to get this job done so that I can *stop* spending time with you."

She laughed. "Your entire goal is to not spend any more

time in prison. And if you wanted to achieve that objective, then maybe you should stop fucking me, stop dicking around with your little two bit-friends, and get your ass back to Geier."

She went back inside and he didn't follow her, even when the cold started seeping through his socks. Only when the front door slammed did he go back in. He breathed a sigh of relief and went into the bathroom for mouthwash. Time get the cigarettes out of his system.

Peregrine: About the Tie

Peri was awake before her first alarm vibrated against her pillow. That wasn't surprising. She frequently woke up sweating and reaching for her knife whenever her neighbor, who worked the night shift, came home and slammed his car door. She never could quite make it back to sleep after that. She turned off the alarm and, moving quietly, took the pile of clothes off the pull-up bar on her closet and rolled the fifteen-pound dumbbells out from under the bed. She cued up her favorite playlist and put her earphones in. Silent burpees had become somewhat of specialty as she had to land softly to avoid rattling the floor. Her mother's room was on the opposite side of the house, and after waking up she usually headed straight for the shower, but it paid to be cautious. Peri worked hard to maintain the illusion of conformity. Conformity maintained anonymity. Anonymity was safety.

Completing her workout, she returned the room to original condition and dressed for breakfast.

The second alarm went off as she was brushing her hair, shoving it into the usual loose braid behind her right ear. She was pulling on her shoes when her mom knocked on the door. Peri froze and considered her next move. This was a violation of routine. She still had twenty minutes before she was expected downstairs for breakfast. "Come in," she called.

"Hey honey." Her mother poked her head in. "The commute is looking extra crappy today with this snow, so I'm leaving early. I can drive you now if you're ready to go."

"Oh." Peri pretended to think about it. "No, I was going to finish up some homework before school. I'll take the bus. But thanks."

"Well, OK. I bought more Eggos at the store, so you're stocked up for breakfast."

"Thanks Mom! Drive carefully."

Her mother smiled benignly as she closed the door. Peri waited until she was out of the house before changing into the Sacred Heart uniform and dialing up a Lyft. Otto wasn't available today, but Kara was. Kara was a single mom, with a baby who only napped in the car, so she doubled up her morning nap hours with driving. She was another one of Peri's favorites, partially because she also didn't mind making extra pit stops. Peri was totally going to stop and get coffee.

The crew was loading something into cars when she arrived at the bowling alley. She chose not to look too closely. She pushed through the front doors and looked for Shark. He came out of the office in his usual button-down with the sleeves rolled up and the collar unbuttoned, which she thought was probably his casual boss look. As far as she was concerned it was his casual hot boss look.

He gave her the once-over. "Oh my God."

Peri looked down at her carefully rumpled disguise, suddenly self-conscious. "Not what you were expecting?"

Domingo walked by and nearly tripped over his feet. "What are you—the worst strippergram ever?"

"Miss Universe contestant. You're not seeing it?"

Chuckling, Domingo carried his box out to the cars.

"It's an all-girls school," Peri reminded Shark, handing him the coffee she'd brought. "The majority of the girls don't bother to dress up. Why would they?"

Shark took a cautious sip. "Sure, makes total sense. I just wasn't expecting it. Won't the teachers wonder who you are?" He smiled at his coffee. She wished he'd smile at her that way.

"You do know I'm not actually going to classes, right?" She ran a hand through her hair, making it even more messy.

Domingo came back in. "Seriously, that's the worst Catholic schoolgirl outfit ever," he said.

She rolled her eyes. "That's because it's an actual Catholic school uniform."

He looked perplexed.

"I hate to ruin the fantasy D, but unless two inches of knee really does it for you, Catholic schoolgirls aren't really sexy."

"Way harsh, bruh," said Domingo, shaking his head as he went back into the kitchen for another load of boxes.

"Are we ready to go?" she asked Shark, who was still sharing a romantic moment with the coffee.

"Yes," he said firmly, refocusing. "Marko is dropping you off. I'm doing the pick-up. Cerise texted me. She should be here momentarily. Everything is set."

Peri tugged at the hem of her untucked shirt. "OK." Cerise

was her favorite local hacker. Her presence made Peri feel more confident that everything would go right.

He pulled a thumb drive out of his pocket. "She prepped this for you."

"Great." She tucked it under her shirt and into the waist belt where she kept her knife sheathed.

"You can still back out," he said suddenly. "We can find a different way, if you don't want to do this."

Her look suggested that he'd lost his mind. "This is a cake walk. It's going to be fine."

"Yeah, of course," he said.

She felt a spurt of unease. What if he wasn't telling her everything? "Where is this coming from? Is there something else I need to know about?"

"No. I just... Fowler may look like a putz, but he's got a mean streak. Honestly, I don't really want him anywhere near you."

She smiled. Marko emerged from the kitchen. His hair was slicked back as usual, but today he was wearing what Peri guessed was his approximation of a dad look—golf shirt and slacks. It was pretty good, but only if he took off the shoulder holster.

"Is Peri—great, you're here. I need five minutes and then I'm good to go."

"Meet you out front," she said.

"Outfit looks great, by the way," said Marko, giving a thumbs-up before retreating back into the kitchen.

"Well, at least some people appreciate my disguise skills." She shouldered her bag and headed for the door, inwardly debating whether or not to add another reassuring comment. Peri looked back and saw that Shark was wearing a peculiar expression, as if he'd just noticed something off. Instinctively, she ran a hand down the back of her skirt.

"What? Did you just figure out that two inches of knee really does it for you?"

"Yes, you caught me," he said. "I don't know if it's the crappy sneakers or the untucked shirt." She envied his ability to keep a straight face. "Or maybe it's the oversized sweater or the badly-tied tie, but I am *so* into it."

"Badly tied…" Peri's hand groped instinctively for her tie and she inspected it on the mirrored side of the claw machine game. "I was aiming for sloppy, not *doesn't know how to tie a tie*. Doesn't know how to tie a tie would be a dead giveaway!"

"*Do* you know how to tie a tie?" Now he really was laughing at her.

"No! I cobbled it together from the diagram that came with the tie!" She tugged ineffectually at the offending length of green material. "I had an actual Catholic schoolgirl do the last one. I never really learned. Stop laughing and help me."

"I'm helping, I'm helping!" He put his coffee on top of the machine, spun her away from the mirror. He gently undid the tie. She waited patiently while he corrected her disaster, enjoying the feeling of his fingers as they occasionally brushed up against her skin. He tied the tie neatly and correctly, and then wiggled it loose. Unexpectedly one of his hands slid up to her face and into her hair. She had a moment of panic as his finger grazed the scar behind her ear, but he didn't notice. All she could do was stare into his amazing gray eyes.

He was going to kiss her. Yes? Please, yes.

"I was trying," he said, "to figure out how you got to be so cool."

Someone was coming. He automatically reached for his coffee with one hand and checked his phone with the other; she returned to adjusting her tie. Domingo went by whistling and carrying a crate.

Peri decided that she fucking hated Domingo like no other.

"OK," said Marko, coming out of the kitchen dusting off his hands. "I'm ready to go."

"Let's do this," said Peri.

Peregrine: The Sacred Heart Gig

Peri strolled onto campus and went directly for the student center. Passing two teachers, she smiled, but avoided eye contact. They barely nodded, deep in conversation. So far, so good.

Hannah was waiting nervously for her at the upper entrance to the student center. Hannah was fifteen and shared her older sister's auburn colored hair and freckles. It had yet to be determined if she shared Sarah's unflappable demeanor. But, by the end of today's mission, Peri figured she'd have the answer one way or another.

"Hey," said Peri. "Is everything in place?"

"Yes, but the girls want to be paid up front," Hannah said. "Is that a problem?" She looked relieved as Peri pulled three fifties out of her pocket. "Sorry, I'm so nervous. It's just this is the first time I've done this without Sarah."

"How's she doing at college, by the way?"

"Good, I think," said Hannah, visibly settling at the mention of her older sister. "I called to get her advice. She said as long as we stuck to the plan it should be easy."

"That's the goal. And remember, if for some reason it does go tits-up, I take the heat and you all walk away." Hannah looked as though she would protest. "I'm equipped for it. And I can't use you again if you get caught."

Hannah tucked a strand of loose hair behind her ear and gave a tiny nod. "This way then."

Emily and Tara were waiting for them downstairs in the lunch room. Peri shook hands, palming them each a fifty. They both messed up the hand-off of the bills and then looked embarrassed. Peri pretended not to notice.

"He just arrived," Emily informed her. Emily was Asian and looked like she'd purposefully tried to look like an anime version of a Catholic schoolgirl. "The teachers are showing him where to put his things. Then they'll take him around to introduce him to the rest of the panel."

"OK, I have the matching bag." Peri hoisted the duplicate laptop bag that Shark had equipped her with. "As we discussed, I'm going to need you to screen me as I do the swap."

"I'm the primary screen," said Emily.

"Good. And if he approaches, who's running interference?"

"That's my job," said Tara. "I'll use the lacrosse maneuver." Tara was a brunette who looked as rumpled as Peri.

Peri nodded approvingly. "Good choice. Hannah, you're the lookout, you give me the sign when I'm cleared to approach. From there I'll exit to the restroom. I need at least twenty minutes, and I'll need a lookout at that location."

"That's me again," said Hannah. "We'll probably have to stay in the bathroom for the entire hour because the entrance is directly opposite the speakers' table. You'll be spotted if you leave." She pointed to the hallway where the bathroom sign and door could clearly be seen. Peri nodded.

"After the talk," said Hannah, "we'll have a line-up of people ready to go to the bathroom. Getting out of here won't be a problem. There's usually an open chat session afterwards when the speakers circulate. That's the best opportunity for putting the bag back."

"Good." Peri smiled at the girls. "This is going to be a snap. You're going to be great. Let's get into position."

Tara and Peri loitered against the wall of the lunchroom, waiting for the others to get into position. It gave Peri ample opportunity to observe Agent Fowler. Just as at the bowling alley, he seemed like he was striving for a look that he wasn't quite capable of pulling off. His tie was too shiny. His physique wasn't quite modelesque. But he had that quality she'd seen in a lot of Adderall users—the ability to seem fun. He glad-handed the teachers, energetically talking to anyone around him, a smile fixed on his face. But she watched his eyes stray from the teacher's face to a student's ass as she bent over to pick up a fallen pen.

At Hannah's signal, Peri started her approach. Emily walked a parallel course and then Tara joined her, pretending to have a conversation, effectively obscuring Fowler's view of his bag. Peri neared the table, barely breaking stride as she made the swap and continued across the room.

She gave Hannah a nod as she passed her and they headed for the bathroom. Glancing back, she saw Emily and Tara take seats at the far back. Everything was going according to plan.

Once inside the restroom, Peri left Hannah by the sinks, locked herself in the handicap stall, and sat on the toilet tank, her feet up on the seat. Booting up, she was faced with a password log-in. She plugged the thumb drive into the USB port, popped her Bluetooth earpiece in, and dialed Cerise.

"I've plugged in," she said when Cerise picked up.

"Yup, I can see it rolling. The screen should go black in a minute and after that I'll have remote access. Just keep the laptop open while I do my shit. How long do we have?"

"If everything goes OK, about an hour."

"Plenty of time," said Cerise. "I'll scoop his hard drive and then we'll have live access to his email."

"Buzz me if you need me," said Peri and hung up.

Setting the laptop down gently, she joined Hannah by the door. Hannah had wedged a stopper between the door and the frame, leaving a two-inch gap that they could listen and watch through.

The teacher was giving the introduction. This was part of their ongoing series on government careers, blah, blah, blah. Peri zoned out as the nun yapped away. She checked her phone. And then social media.

"And aren't we lucky," said the nun hitting a register that penetrated Peri's fog, "that Agent Fowler volunteered his time to talk about the ATF?"

"Volunteered?" repeated Peri . Hannah shrugged.

When Agent Fowler finally took the stage, his speech was a mix of historical facts about the ATF, humblebrag anecdotes, and useless safety tips. Peri had to admit that he was good, entertaining, connected to the audience, oozing the right amount of charming adultness.

About halfway through, Hannah whispered, "He's off, isn't he?" He seems right, but there's something just a little…"

"Skeezebag?" suggested Peri.

"Yeah." Hannah looked puzzled. Maybe this was the first time she'd encountered one in the wild. "Why don't they see it?" she asked, gesturing at the nuns.

"It's hard to see when you're a part of the crowd," said Peri. "You have to take a step back. And you know adults—they don't see what they don't want to see."

The speech was starting to wind down when Cerise texted: I'M OUT. BOOK YOUR RETURN FLIGHT.

The screen had returned to the log-in. She folded it closed and returned it to the bag.

When she emerged from the stall, Hannah had started to tense up. "We're almost at the free chat period," she said. "Once Sister Dolores releases everyone there will be a bunch who come to the bathroom. We can leave then."

They got a few odd looks from the first group to hit the bathroom, but then they were out the door and no one looked twice. Most of the girls were gathered around the cookie table, but Fowler was chatting up some of the students, and of course standing between her and the chair with his bag on it.

"We walk straight by," said Peri to Hannah. "Emily and Tara, run the screen behind us."

The girls nodded.

"You two go right," said Hannah. "Come in from the side. We don't want to look like a herd. We'll give you a head start."

The delay of waiting for Emily and Tara to get into position gave Peri another chance to watch Fowler. High school had a pecking order. Girls who could dress right and had mastered social skills were at the top. The shy ones, the ones that couldn't quite fit in, they were always at the bottom. Fowler was talking to those. She felt a qualm as they started their approach. He seemed too aware of the crowd around him.

They were about to pass when Fowler looked up. "Did you enjoy the speech? Please say yes. My ego is on the line here."

One of the other girls giggled nervously. "Um, yeah," said Peri. "It was great. Hannah, can you put my bag back for me?" She handed the bag to Hannah and stepped closer to Fowler, pulling his attention to her and away from his bag. "I thought your safety tips were really interesting. It's hard to know where to feel safe these days."

"Isn't it, though," said Fowler, smiling. There was more eye contact. Peri could feel him intentionally focusing on her. She thought the next thing he would do was touch her in some way—nothing inappropriate, just something to build a connection. Behind him Tara and Emily moved smoothly into place as Hannah passed them.

"Maybe you'd be interested in this place?" He held out a card. A blue logo read HAPPY PLACE YOUTH CENTER. "It's a really great kids' center." She glanced around—all the girls held similar cards. He touched her hand briefly and then pointed to the logo. "I was just telling some of the other girls about it." She felt her heart stop as she saw a black tattoo briefly flash above the edge of his cuff. She caught a brief glimpse of what looked very much like a portion of the letter Q. Maybe it was nothing. Maybe it was a part of a larger tattoo. Or maybe she knew exactly what it was.

"That's an interesting tattoo," she said, reaching for the shirt sleeve.

He pushed the cuff down to cover the mark, avoiding her. "Learn from my mistakes, kids," he said, flashing his teeth. "Don't let a girl talk you into getting a tattoo when you're drunk. Anyway, you should check out the Happy Place."

Hannah was walking toward the exit, decoy bag in hand. The computer was back in place.

"Oh, thanks, maybe." Peri considered her options. He was carrying—one on his hip and one on his ankle. That would make taking him on difficult. She was in a high school. The nuns were not going to appreciate it if she started slicing pieces off people. But most of all, Fowler belonged to Shark. She couldn't interfere with his plans without making a big mess. And maybe she was wrong. She needed evidence before she could do anything. "I appreciate it," Peri added, backing up. She needed to get out before she did something stupid.

Once outside she slipped Hannah an extra fifty and gave her a hug for a job well done. Then she jogged across the campus to where the softball field was blocked from the road by an eight-foot wall.

It was time to get the hell out of Sacred Heart.

Shark: Sacred Heart

There was a rustle in the trees and he craned his neck, looking up into the trees.

"Oh, seriously?" said Peri from somewhere along the wall. "FML. Why can't I ever look smooth?"

"Peri, what's going on up there?" he asked, trying to see her through the desiccated remains of dried leaves.

"I tried to drop the bag down and the damn thing got stuck on a branch. Hold on."

He finally spotted her crawling out along a bough, toward her backpack. It was a good view. "Pineapples are still my favorite," he said.

"Trying to concentrate up here," she said with a chuckle. The bag dropped down with a thud.

"I was just commenting. How'd it go?"

"Fine." She hung down, lounging against the bark, reminding him of a cat. "Except I think Regan was right."

"Mutually assured destruction is a viable deterrent policy?"

"Regan, my friend on the drill team. That Fowler dude is a pervert." She rolled off the branch and swung down.

He stepped forward to catch her, but the momentum was more than he'd expected and she slithered through his arms until he was left holding her ass. "What makes you think he's a pervert…asks the man with his hands up your skirt."

She laughed and he tried to think non-sex-related thoughts. It wasn't going well. She smelled amazing and she was looking at him with those gold eyes of hers and there was way too much of her body available to him. He set her down gently and she gave a shake to straighten her skirt, avoiding eye contact.

"No one should see me in this outfit. Kids, teachers, everyone—they ought to look right through me. It's what it's designed to do. But Fowler tried to talk to me. I had to call an audible just to get the computer back in place."

"Not every disguise can be a home run. Some people are smarter than they look."

"It wasn't just me. He was targeting everyone who looked like me. He was hunting for the low self-esteemers. And…" She stopped and he waited for whatever she was going to say. Her lips were pursed and she was staring off into the distance. "He handed out a bunch of cards to some sort of youth center," she said, but Shark got the feeling that hadn't been what she was going to say originally.

"So maybe he's a do-gooder?" He had to admit that it sounded implausible even as he said it. He met her cynical look with an apologetic gesture.

"Maybe," said Peri, heading to his car. As always, he opened the passenger door for her. "Or maybe it would just be better for everyone if we can put his ass in jail."

"That is the plan."

"And we're sure you can't just kill him?" she asked seriously.

"You really did *not* like him." She was so cute about murder.

"I don't like abusers," she said simply.

"The clean play is to put him in jail," he said. "But one way or another, he's going down."

"Well," she said, pushing hair out of her face, "then I will stop worrying about him."

"Thanks for the vote of confidence. Are we going back to the bowling alley?"

"Sorry, no. I've got drill team practice. Can you drop me at school?"

He nodded his agreement, as she began to pull off her clothes. He would have accused her of doing it to tantalize, but there wasn't much of a strip tease in her movements. She really seemed to not give a fuck if he saw her naked.

He took a deep breath and reminded himself that he was being professional. She was being professional. They were being professional as fuck. Aside from the kiss in the car, she'd respected his boundaries. The fact that he wished she wouldn't was his problem.

"You switched to a waist holster?" he asked as she pulled her shirt and sweater over her head. Then realized he'd just admitted to looking.

"Thigh holsters are too noticeable in this skirt," she said from under her sweater. "Besides, this one," she dropped the shirt and sweater in her bag, and patted the elastic band around her waist, "can hold two knives."

"I don't think I want to be there for the occasion where you need two knives," he said with a laugh.

Peregrine: Uncle Al at Work

After drill team practice, Peri called a Lyft to get her to the bowling alley, but halfway there she asked Otto to make a detour. He obliged, knowing that her detours always meant generous tips.

"You can wait a minute or two, yeah?" asked Peri.

"I can wait." Otto looked around at the crappy motel parking lot with doubt.

"Great. I'll be right back."

She jogged over to Al's mint-green Bronco and climbed in.

Al glanced up from the camera that was focused on one of the rooms of the motel. "I'm working."

"Nice to see you too."

"I don't have time for whatever this is," he said. "I'm busy."

"Yes, waiting for cheating spouses to stop screwing, who wants to be distracted from that?"

"How did you even know I was here?"

"It's Mrs. Meechem, right? I thought this was her regular three o'clock."

"Apparently, I talk too much," said Al.

"Nah, I go through your notebook when you're not looking." Then she grinned. "Relax, I'm teasing. You mentioned it last week. Anyway, I've got to make this quick. I'm holding up Otto."

"What's an Otto?"

"My Lyft driver. Look, can you do me a favor?"

"Depends on what it is. And how the fuck do you afford a car service? You don't have a job." Al was always a little unclear on her funding and she didn't care to enlighten him.

"Mom does, though," she said, as she handed him the card. Like her mother would pay her Lyft bill. Like her mother even *knew* about her Lyft bill.

"That's a ridiculous waste of money."

"Well, I could get a car, but then you'd have to teach me how to drive. You know, for actual real. Instead of just expecting me to pick you up at a bar."

He glared at her. "I never asked you to do that."

"Your bartenders did, so whatever. Anyway, unless you want to teach me how to use turn signals or something—"

"Isn't that what drivers ed is for?" She was seriously managing to annoy him and that really hadn't been what she was trying for.

"I skipped that so I could take another college course. Meanwhile, can we focus? I heard this guy give a career-day talk." No need to mention at which school. "Afterwards he was really targeting specific girls and pitching this youth center thing. I don't have anything specific on him—it's just a feeling—but I don't think he's right."

"Your instincts are usually pretty good," Al said.

"I've got a pretty good batting average," she agreed. "But we've been assuming that whoever was targeting girls was doing it through social media, but what if they're IRL?" She saw his blank expression. "In real life."

He took the card. "Happy Place," he read. "Who was the guy?"

"An ATF Agent named Fowler. Don't worry about him."

Al's face grew serious. "And why am I not worrying about him? What are you up to?"

"Just the usual dirt," said Peri. "Don't worry about him because he's someone else's problem."

"Whose problem?"

"Not mine and not yours," said Peri.

His fingers tapped out *Shave and a Haircut* on the steering wheel. "Peri, do we need to revisit the ground rules? You're not supposed to be doing anything that could get you dead."

Like that ship hadn't sailed years ago. "Al, seriously—"

"Don't *seriously* me. Are you taking on this Fowler guy?"

"Hand to God, I'm not," said Peri. "Stop spazzing."

Al's eyes narrowed. "OK. *Why* aren't you taking him on?"

"Didn't you just say you didn't want me to?" Peri didn't have to fake her confusion.

"Yeah, and you just told me you didn't want me to. So who is?"

Peri sighed in exasperation. She was really going to have to be more careful if Al stayed sober. He was not nearly this difficult to manage while impaired. "Karma will catch up with him. Stop worrying about him. Focus on the *Happy Place*."

"I am focusing," snapped Al. "What I believe you to be saying is that you think Fowler is involved in sex trafficking, and that instead of pursuing that lead, you would like me to pursue this crappy youth center."

"Yeah, that about covers it," she said, opening the door, preparing to leave. Al had always said the first rule of self-defense was to run away if possible. He probably hadn't meant that principle to apply to conversations with him, but it still worked.

"If I find out you're going after him, I'll confiscate your knives and tell your mom you need therapy," he said.

"You wouldn't dare," gasped Peri, whirling around in the seat.

"What's the matter? Baring your soul to a therapist doesn't sound like much fun? Should I shove another pamphlet at you?"

"You have nightmares!"

"So do you!" he yelled back.

There was a long silence while Peri tried to figure out how to walk the conversation back. "Stay sober and I'll stop with the pamphlets," she offered.

"Don't mess with Fowler and I won't say anything to your mom."

"I really am not going to," she promised.

"OK, fine."

"Fine," agreed Peri. They stared at each other some more. She had been unprepared to either be real or fight with Al this afternoon and she found that she wanted to cry, but she knew that would freak him out. "Otto's waiting for me," she said. "Also, you need to shave."

"I was thinking of just letting the beard happen."

"You're not going hipster just because you stopped drinking, are you?"

"Yes," he said. "A man bun is next. Followed by a porkpie hat."

"What's a porkpie hat?" she asked, relieved to be back on bullshitting terms.

"You know, one of those stupid hats with the brim?" He gestured to indicate general size and shape.

"Like a fedora."

"No, fedoras are cooler. As a private investigator, I'm allowed to wear a fedora. In fact, I'm fairly certain it's in the manual that I have to own one."

"The manual you never read?"

"That's the one," he said. "Your driver's waiting. Hey," he added, before she could leave. "Have you seen my number-four camera?"

Peri cursed internally. "Yeah, I've got it. I'll bring it by later."

"Stop stealing my shit."

"I said I'd bring it back," she said. "That makes it borrowing." Then she slammed the door.

Shark: Rolling Thunder Lanes

Shark was scrolling through his phone and waiting on Cerise when Peri came in, the early winter sunset throwing red light through the door and outlining her figure as she came in. She waved at Marko, who was poking at one of the ball-return machines with a wrench. Cerise peered out from behind the stack of empty coconut water cans piled on the bar next to her computer. Her long braids were worked through with purple, but she was wearing them down instead of piled high on her head, as she had when Shark had first met her.

"Hey girl," said Cerise, standing up.

"Hey!" chirped Peri.

Cerise hugged her, then stretched. "I'm going out for a smoke. When I get back you can explain about the Tupperware."

"Ah, the Tupperware returns," said Shark, as Cerise walked outside. "You make any progress on finding the memory card?"

Peri slapped the container on the bar and wordlessly held up a plastic baggie full of cards of various shapes—it was labeled BASTARDS GET OUT OF MY FACE. Then she held up a baggie full cards that were all the same type. It was labeled MIGHT BE THE ONE. The she held up a slightly less full baggie of cards labeled NOT THE ONE. "Sure," she said. "Progress. How's it going here?"

"Cerise has been doing her thing."

"I can tell," said Peri, gesturing to the empty containers.

"She says any minute now we will have something. Of course, that's any Cerise minute, so I'm estimating sometime within the next half-hour." Peri's eyes twinkled in amusement. "Also, Eddie and Beef found out that we have black lights and are threatening to host a rock and glow bowling night for the gang."

"What the hell is rock and glow?"

"I asked the same thing." He was happy to know he wasn't the only one who hadn't heard of it. "Apparently, you turn out the lights, and just use the black lights and strobes and have glow in the dark balls and pins."

Peri chuckled, her shoulders shaking. "I would pay money to see that."

"I'm sure I could get you an invitation. And let's see what else? Oh, there's that mess over there." He gestured to Marko. "The ball return has stopped working and Marko keeps threatening to shoot the repairman for daring to turn in a quote for what I personally consider to be a reasonable amount." Peri giggled and began to divest herself of her jacket and bag. "Supposedly, Domingo is helping with that project, but secretly I think he's crashing in the storeroom."

Peri wrinkled her nose in unhappiness. "His mom's boyfriend is an asshole."

"That is the impression I got," said Shark. He didn't mention the welts he'd seen on Domingo's back a few months ago. Paper had said that Domingo put up with it to stop the boyfriend from going after his younger siblings. Shark was all too familiar with the math of abuse and was keeping out of it for now.

"Are you going to let him stay?" she asked.

"As long as he doesn't drink the liquor it's fine with me." That earned him a smile.

There was a string of profanity from Marko, followed by a sharp thunk.

"Domingo," he bellowed, "hit it."

The ball-return machine whirred to life and Domingo came out of the back room. "Hey Peri." He yelled at Marko, "Did that do it?"

Marko sent a bowling ball down the lane and they all watched in anticipation as the ball disappeared into the return, then popped back out like candy from a Pez dispenser.

"Yeah!" yelled Domingo just as Cerise came back in. She looked entertained at the rousing welcome, and Domingo blushed.

"Fucking kids and their fucking bubble gum," said Marko, toting his bag of tools.

"Hey, we haven't done anything to piss off the Vagos, have we?" asked Paper, walking in the front door behind Cerise.

Marko paused and glanced at Shark. Peri deliberately didn't, keeping her face impassive. Shark wished he could train his guys to do the same.

"Not anything recently," replied Shark. "Why?"

"Two of them just cruised the building. Real slow. Didn't like the look of it."

Paper might not be the sharpest pencil in the drawer, but his street instincts were good. "Call someone in," Shark ordered.

"Put a lookout on the door. With Fowler on our ass, we don't have any room for extra bullshit."

Paper nodded, already dialing his phone as he headed for the kitchen, Domingo following. Shark wondered if he should do something about his ever increasing food bill. The kitchen seemed to be the first stop for anyone in the gang that came in. On the other hand, some of the kids didn't look like they got a decent meal anywhere else and Marko seemed to make a point of keeping sandwiches on hand.

"All right," said Cerise, finishing off a coconut water, "bathroom break and then we'll see what we've got."

Peri took a seat, and began sifting through the loose chips. Shark took the seat next to her, grabbed a handful, and began sorting too. "This is the magic, isn't it?" he asked.

"What?" she stared at him blankly.

"Domingo and the guys think that you wave your magic wand and make magic happen. Poof! You've got a Sacred Heart uniform."

"Ah," said Peri, realization dawning. "Yeah, every magic trick starts with a shit-ton of practice and preparation."

"Or in this case, sorting through about a thousand memory cards. Are you going to tell me what's on it when we do find it?"

"Probably not," said Peri, reaching over him to grab another handful. Her arm brushed up against his and he tried not to read into it. "This particular magic trick isn't for you."

"Well, I figured. Never let them see you sweat, right?"

"Exactly," she said. Cerise came back and eyed the Tupperware project and shook her head.

"I changed my mind. I don't want to know what that mess is," she said, taking her seat in front of the computer again. Peri laughed.

"Hey," she said as Cerise began to type, "have you heard of something called Happy Place?"

"Yeah," Cerise answered without looking up. "Some shitty youth center after school place."

"You ever hear of anything sketchy going down there?"

Cerise frowned, thinking. "No, I don't think so, why?"

"Fowler was pushing it today after his talk, and something about him was… Pervtastic, I guess. Just made me suspicious."

Marko came out of the kitchen with his rosemary garlic fries and put them down on the bar.

"Vegetable oil," he said to Cerise. "Totally vegetarian friendly."

Cerise beamed, grabbing a handful. "He's a molester type? I can search for that. I mean, I've got his hard drive contents. You want me to look?"

"I would love you to, but your time is not my dime," said Peri. She and Cerise turned to Shark hopefully.

Marko burst out laughing. "Good luck saying no to that," he advised Shark.

"I don't have to say no," said Shark. "All dirt on Fowler is good for me."

"Great." Cerise's fingers were already flying across the keyboard.

His phone buzzed. Vivian's number. "Be right back," he said, taking the phone into the office.

"Trying to work over here," he greeted Vivian.

"Yeah, well you've been working too hard," she said. "They're about to bust you for killing Fred Abernathy. What the fuck did you do?"

Shark laughed.

"You think this is funny? If you get caught for killing someone while on FBI payroll, I go down too. And if I'm going down I will make sure you never fucking see the sun again."

"Relax," he said. "I'm not going to get popped for Abernathy. When are they coming?"

"Now. They're also serving search warrants on your friends Paper, Marko, and Eddie."

"Beef is going to be hurt," he said. Eddie and Beef were best friends, but always seemed to compete. This was going to put Eddie one up on search warrants.

"Shark, I swear to God—"

"I've got to go. Bye." He left the office. "Everybody out," he told them. "Grab your things. Leave nothing. Cops are on their way."

"Cops again? They can't possibly have anything." Marko looked pissed.

"They want to question me about Fred Abernathy."

Paper and Marko both looked nervous. Cerise and Peri didn't even exchange glances. God, he loved working with professionals.

"I also suggest not going back to your places. They have search warrants out on you two and Eddie." He pointed at Marko and Paper.

"Beef is going to be pissed," said Marko. "What? He's not cool enough to search?"

"Let 'em look," said Paper. "I cleaned out my place just like you said. And Abernathy was never even there, so fuck them."

"Still might not want to go home for a bit." He unholstered his gun and handed it to Marko. "Cerise, I'll be in touch. Don't call until you hear from me or Marko."

"Yeah, OK. But, well you might want to see this. It just came in." Cerise spun the laptop around so he could see the email: LOCATION AND TIME CONFIRMED. MERCHANDISE HAD BETTER BE THERE. NO MORE DELAYS.

Shark sighed. "Never enough time," he said. "OK, look into that. I'll be in contact." She nodded, already packing up. "Peri, Marko can give you a ride."

"Sure. Sounds good." She shoveled all the chips into the Tupperware and grabbed her bag.

"You want me to call Williamson?" asked Marko, pulling on his jacket.

"I'll do it after you're all out," said Shark. "And I'll have him call you if there's anything that needs to be done."

Marko made a final check of the area and shepherded his charges out the door.

Shark waited until they were gone and then placed two calls. By the time the cops arrived he was ready. The cops, however, did not appear to be in a mood to get anything done. Five hours in holding followed by two hours in interrogation had passed before he was allowed to see his lawyer.

"This is outrageous," said Taylor Williamson, bursting into

the room. "You have specifically blocked access to my client and I will be filing a complaint!" He was dressed in a chunky sweater and a Gucci scarf. Shark wished he could hate on it, but the lawyer looked good.

Williamson shooed the cops out of the room and Shark heard more outrage and threats from the other side of the door before the lawyer came back in and sat down.

"So," he began. "They have evidence placing you in the home of an accountant named Fred Abernathy."

"OK," said Shark.

Williamson appeared to be parsing Shark's lack of panic. "Mr. Abernathy has not been heard from in several months."

"Yes," said Shark.

Williamson's eyebrows went up. "They want to pin his death on you," he said, as if Shark didn't grasp the implications.

"I got what you were saying the first time," said Shark. "I got it the first 700 times they asked me where I was on the night of whenever that was. I'm not confused. I just don't answer any questions without a lawyer present."

"Good policy," said Williamson. "So you have an alibi?" He looked hopeful, pen poised over his notepad.

"No, I was at his house."

Williamson's nose twitched. "We seem to be talking at cross purposes. Perhaps you would care to tell me what happened to Fred Abernathy?"

"Nothing happened. He's not dead. He's in Utah."

"I've been to Utah," said Williamson. "It is my impression that death may be somewhat similar. Can you prove his whereabouts?"

"I've got his phone number," said Shark.

Williamson pushed the notepad over to him. "Write it down. This is going to be so much fun." He waved in the cops, who entered warily, like wolves who'd just gotten a cheerful hello from a bunny. "My client has agreed to answer questions about Fred Abernathy," he told them.

The detectives exchanged looks. The skinny one with the beady eyes sat down across from him.

"Do you deny knowing Fredrick Abernathy?"

Williamson gave him the nod. "I know Fred," said Shark.

"What was your relationship with Fredrick Abernathy?"

Another nod from Williamson. "He was my accountant for a short period of time."

"Do you deny that you have been inside Abernathy's residence?"

A Williamson nod. "No."

"Do you have knowledge of Abernathy's current whereabouts?"

Shark looked at Williamson, who slid the notepad across the table. "This is Mr. Abernathy's current number," said Williamson. "At this point, we suggest you direct your questions to Mr. Abernathy himself."

"You know what?" said Skinny. "I'll play along." He took out his phone and entered the number, hit the speaker button, and laid it on the table. It rang loudly in the quiet room. On the fifth ring, just when Shark was beginning to sweat, Fred picked up.

"Ahoy-hoy," he answered. "You've got Captain Fred." From the sounds on the other end of the line, Captain Fred was in the midst of a party.

The detectives looked shocked. "Um, hello, is this Fred Abernathy?" asked Skinny.

"Yeah, who's this?"

"Hey Fred," said Shark, jumping in before the detectives could recover. "This is Shark. The police have arrested me for killing you."

Fred burst out laughing. He was playing it beautifully.

"Sir," said Plump Detective, forcefully moving the phone away from Shark, "can you describe your relationship with Mr. Santoyo? How did you meet?"

"Work. I was doing some accounting for a guy named Paul Paulson and he ran off with some start-up capital on this bowling alley. Shark came into town to try and get the bowling alley back on its feet for the owner. Shark, how did that go?"

"Oh, it took a little longer than expected, but we're finally open."

"That's great!"

"Never mind that," said Skinny. "Did Mr. Santoyo make you leave town or harm you in any way?"

"What? Oh, gosh no! After my divorce, I was just really bummed out. Shark talked me off the ledge. Convinced me to come back out here to be with my family. Best decision I've made lately."

"How do we know that you're really Fred Abernathy?" asked Plump.

"Uh…" In the background on Fred's end of the phone call, they could all hear girls laughing. "Oh, here, I know. Shark, are you still at the same number?"

"Yeah," said Shark.

"Hold on just a minute," said Fred. Moments later Shark's phone pinged with multiple incoming texts. "Cindy may have gotten a little carried away on that last one."

Shark pulled up the texts and turned it around to face the detectives. He scrolled through three selfies where Fred's face could clearly be seen. Also, Cindy's breasts, but mostly Fred's face.

"Thanks Fred," said Shark. "That ought to do it."

"OK," Fred said cheerfully. "Glad I could help! Bye!"

Williamson reached over and hung up the detective's phone. "Soooo," he said. "I expect all charges to be dropped. And if any of you so much as breathe in my client's direction we'll be suing for harassment."

"Harassment? Your client is a thug," said Skinny.

"No, my client is a parolee out on good behavior, who is trying to turn his life around by becoming a small businessman."

"He's employing half the gangbangers in town!"

"They're gaining valuable job skills," Shark said. "I like to give back to the community."

"He's trying to give others the opportunities that he never got. This, combined with the beating he received from the vice squad a few weeks ago, shows a clear pattern of harassment.

Come near him again and not only will I have your badges, we will be suing the city for damages." Williamson stood, tossed his scarf over his shoulder and exited the room with a step that was barely short of a flounce.

Shark stood up and prepared to follow. "Sorry, guys. Better luck next time."

Shark: The Condo

By the time he made it back to the condo it was nearly three in the morning. Marko and Paper were sitting on his couch playing *Call of Duty*. Domingo was passed out in an armchair, his feet on the coffee table. Eddie sat leafing through one of Shark's copies of *Dwell*. At this stage of the evening, Eddie's thick, black hair had broken free of its pomade and was sticking up.

"This is a good magazine," said Eddie. "These houses are crazy."

"Hey," said Marko, pausing the game. "What's the word? We never heard from Williamson."

"No need," said Shark. "They don't have anything. I was released."

They all looked suitably impressed. Only Marko looked suspicious. "You must be one lucky bastard," he said.

"Anyway," Shark said, "I'm good and you guys are also in the clear. You can go home."

"I think he's trying to give us a hint," grunted Eddie. He caught sight of his reflection in the window and smoothed his hair back down.

Marko slipped his shoes on. "Well, someone needs to kick Domingo then."

Paper put the controllers back in their basket under the

coffee table and shook Domingo. They straggled out the door, Marko the last to leave.

"Thanks for looking out for the kids," Shark told him. He really did appreciate Marko's steadying influence. Most of his crew were under twenty-one and had a tendency to do stupid-ass shit when an adult wasn't present. Without Marko, he probably would have returned to a full-fledged party in his living room.

Marko snorted. "I love how you say *kids* like you're not one of them."

Shark scrutinized Marko's wide Italian face. He'd spent a fair portion of his career punching people who thought he was too young to be a threat; he knew he had a short fuse on the subject, but it got boring, having to explain that age didn't make him less capable of doing his job or less capable of shooting someone in the fucking face. It had been a relief to come out of prison and find that those comments had mostly ceased. Which made this one a bit of a surprise. Marko had never previously given him shit about his age. Shark wasn't sure what to make of it.

Zipping his coat Marko said, "I know, I know, you're not in the same league. You've been running with the big boys since you were in diapers. I'm just saying, from this side of thirty-five, you all look like fucking babies to me."

"Well, in that case, what I mean to say is thanks for looking out for my apartment. It's nice to know that I've got at least a sixty percent chance of still having beer in my fridge."

Marko chuckled. "I did send Eddie out to get a refill. I think Domingo has a hollow leg."

"It's not just me? I swear that kid drinks beer like it's Seven-Up."

"It's not just you. I told him to cut back. He's going to stunt his growth."

Shark laughed and then yawned.

"Oh," said Marko, opening the door, but turning back at the last minute. "I forgot to mention. You might want to keep it down. Peri's in the bed."

"What? Why?" Shark felt a spike of adrenaline and tried to mask the emotion in his voice. "You were taking her home."

"She said she needed a space to go through all the chips." Marko pointed to the kitchen table where the camera and the bags of cards were sitting. "Then she got done and said she was going to take a nap. She never came back out. I mean, you can kick her out if you want." His eyes crinkled in laughter.

"Go away," said Shark, tiredly.

"Yes, boss."

Shark poured himself a drink, made a sandwich. The cards in the Tupperware had all been subdivided into their bags, including a new bag containing a single chip that read: THE ONE. On impulse he put it into the camera and pushed play.

On the tiny screen, the video showed a roadway, and the tall struts of what was probably an overpass. Fast forwarding, he realized that the camera must have been motion-activated as the image cut from birds, to cars, to homeless people. He slowed it down for what was clearly a drug buy. Good-sized bulk, but not his guys. He made a mental note of the makes and models of the cars. Other than that, he couldn't see what Peri wanted with the footage.

He put the card back in the baggie and ate his sandwich, pondering what to do about Peri. He hated sharing his bed. One of the luxuries of having money and of not being in fucking prison was a large bed and hearing only his own breathing at the end of the night. If he wasn't getting laid, he just wasn't sure it was worth it.

The bedroom door was locked, because apparently her trust of his crew only went so far. He didn't blame her. He got the lock picks out of his kit, feeling a little silly. The lock was so flimsy he really didn't need them. But on the other hand, he had no intention of damaging his own door.

She was curled up in the upper left corner of the bed as if afraid to take up space. The Glock he kept under the mattress was on the bedside table, next to her knife. He tried not to find that endearing. He went into the bathroom and when he came back out, she still hadn't moved. He could see her pulse beating in her throat, her hair was a tangled mess on the pillow, and for the first time he noticed that the hollows under her eyes were a smudgy purple. Maybe she needed the sleep as much as he did. Still, he wondered if he should wake her up and take her home. Seventeen and eight months was a lot closer to eighteen than he'd previously estimated her to be, but it didn't change any of the other factors. Or the existence of the perfect Stanford-bound boyfriend who couldn't possibly appreciate her the way she deserved.

He gingerly lifted the covers and checked the dress code. She was wearing a t-shirt and underwear. On her hip, he could see the faintest scar as if she'd been cut at some point. He stripped down to his underwear, climbed in, and lay there waiting for her breathing to annoy him. Instead it just seemed rhythmic and re-assuring. The light from the windows outlined her body.

Outside, a truck trundled by, the wheels clunking against a pothole. Peri started, stretched out and then rolled over. He breathed in the scent of her shampoo and realized what a mistake this was. He should take her home. He *would* take her home. Because if she stayed he wasn't going to remember that there were reasons why she shouldn't.

He closed his eyes and listened to her breathing. Maybe he could wait just a little longer?

Thursday ~ December 29

Peregrine: Swing and a Miss

She woke up with her face mashed into Shark's shoulder and her knee draped over his stomach. Everywhere they were touching was hot and sweaty. She pulled herself off and rolled away, struggling with the hair that immediately fell into her face.

Shark's eyes were open now and he was very obviously amused. She felt unreasonably embarrassed and sank down into the covers until only her eyes showed. "Stop laughing at me," she said.

With one finger he pulled the duvet away from her face. "Are you going to stop being funny?"

She tried to think of a response. She was not good at being witty in the morning. "I don't hear the guys. Where is everyone?"

"They left when I got home," he said. "Around three."

"Around three? Why didn't you wake me up?"

"I didn't want to get shot?" he suggested.

She twisted her head to look at his gun on the bedside table next to her knife.

"Or stabbed. You know, whatever came first."

"Sorry, I wasn't trying to crash. But I needed a nap. And the gun was making a lump."

"Such a princess," he said, shaking his head.

She chuckled. "But didn't you want your bed back? I don't know about you, but every time I spend the night with someone I end up sleepless and annoyed."

"They always do all that breathing," he agreed.

"And they hog the covers," she added.

"And the middle of the bed. Stick to your own side!" Under the covers, with one quick move he pulled her closer, leaning over her. She felt a thrill of anticipation in her stomach. She slid her hands up his arms, enjoying the warmth of his skin. She had a moment of panic wondering about morning breath, but then he was kissing her, and everything else was forgotten.

As he kissed her neck she let out a soft moan and felt herself arch up into him. Everything he did seemed to set her skin on fire. Nothing felt awkward or clumsy like it did with Trey. She quickly pushed thoughts of Trey out of her head and concentrated on what Shark's hands were doing. She had the simultaneous urge to make him speed up and slow down. She nibbled his earlobe and slid one hand down the length of his back. He worked her shirt up. She slid one hand under the edge of his underwear. They were both breathing heavily and she could tell her efforts were having an impact on him when she became aware of an annoying ringing noise.

"God, make your alarm stop or I swear I'll break your phone," she gasped.

He laughed. "I'm pretty sure that's yours."

Peri felt a sudden chill. "Shit." She pushed him off and floundered, trying to escape the bed. "Shit. Shit, shit, shit!" She leapt out of the bed, looking for her bag, scrabbled through its pockets looking for her phone. She slammed it off and tried not to hyperventilate.

"Peri," he said, sitting up. "Forget about school. Come back to bed."

"School? Who gives a shit about school? That's second alarm." She looked around wildly for her pants. Surely she had come in with pants.

"I don't know what that means," he said, scrubbing at his temple with one hand. Naturally, he was detestably cute in the morning.

"It means that my mother is expecting me at the breakfast table in twenty-five minutes!" she yelped and flung herself into the bathroom.

She ran a brush through her hair and came back out to find him pulling on pants, muttering, "This would be a whole lot easier if you would stop being so fucking hot"

Peri had never once heard herself described as *fucking hot*. She knew that when she made an effort she wasn't unattractive, but somehow *fucking hot* had never been applied to her. She kissed him. It seemed like the only appropriate response, but his rebuttal was to pull her back onto the bed. Three precious minutes later, she managed to separate.

"No," she said, pointing at him like he'd been a bad dog. "No. We do not have time for this." He smiled at her, a slow smile that tested her resolve. Her finger closed back into a fist.

"Mmmph!" she growled in angry frustration and backed away. "I do not need this right now."

"Are you sure?"

She was sure she wanted his hands all over her body. She was absolutely sure about that.

"Pants," she said. "I need pants."

"On the chair."

By the time she arrived at the door she felt she'd run a mile. Shark on the other hand looked cool as a cucumber and was already waiting for her there, flipping his keys in and out of his hand. "How'd you do that?" she asked.

"Haste is the enemy of speed," he said.

"Fuck you, Confucius."

He grinned. "I live here. I know where my pants are."

"We're not going to my house first," she said as they got in to his car. "I can't sneak into the house. Mom's already up. I have to make it look like I left early. I'm going with the jogging protocol." She directed him to Uncle Al's.

Ten minutes later Shark pulled up behind Al's Bronco. "Wait here," said Peri and sprinted up the stairs, pulling off her jacket as she went. Inside she threw down her jacket, grabbed the duffle bag out of the hall closet, shed her clothes and pulled on her jogging tights and sweatshirt. She was lacing her running shoes when Al came out of his bedroom.

"Jogging protocol," she yelled and sprinted out again.

"Whose place was that?" Shark wanted to know.

"Forget that place. It's just where I keep clothes."

"Mm."

When he dropped her off, a block from her house, she kissed him with as much passion as she thought she could get away without moving matters to the backseat and left him with a bemused expression on his face. Running up to the house she tossed her backpack into the garage and jogged into the kitchen. At least she didn't have to fake sweat.

"Hey honey," Her mom looked surprised. "I was just about to call you down. Were you out jogging?"

Peri went to the refrigerator. "Yeah, I went running with Uncle Al."

"Oh, honey, I wish you wouldn't do that. He's not... well."

"He's an alcoholic, Mom. You can just say it."

"Well, yes, he is. And that's why I don't like you going out with him. I don't think it's safe."

Her mother leaned against the counter, waiting for the microwave to finish zapping her 250 calories of cardboard instant breakfast.

Peri poured a glass of orange juice. "Actually, he can't drink while he runs. So it's a healthy behavior for him, and having him there makes it safer for me."

Her mother nodded thoughtfully. As usual, she looked elegant. She'd managed the nearly impossible feat of stylish cold-weather office wear, with a heavy sweater dress over tights. Peri knew that her snow boots would be swapped out for heels once she reached her office in the city. Her carefully tinted and coifed hair always made Peri wonder where the genes had gone wrong. How could her mother's hair look like a shampoo commercial while hers always looked like she'd been rolling around in bed twenty minutes ago?

Peri took a moment to enjoy the fact that she really had been rolling around in bed twenty minutes ago.

"Besides," said Peri, turning back to the fridge to hide the smile creeping onto her face, "if I want to be on the drill team I've got to get in shape."

"I'm really excited about the drill team opportunity for you. I think it's a great extra-curricular. Can't hurt the college application. Plus it's an opportunity for you to make new friends."

Peri refrained from stating that she didn't want new friends.

"Particularly now that Trey has moved to California."

"Yeah, maybe."

"Well, anyway, if it turns out to be something you want to pursue, maybe we can get you a gym membership. You know, to one of those fun new cross-training places."

Peri refrained from mentioning that she'd belonged to a gym for the last four years. Admittedly, it was a gym populated by people that made Al look well-adjusted, but they were the ones who had the skills she needed.

"Yeah, I'll think about it," she replied, trying to sound genuine. She could sense her mom making an effort to reach out. She just didn't know how to reach back.

Shark: Southern Roots Cafe

After leaving Peri, Shark texted Cerise. She replied that she'd meet him for breakfast at some dive he'd never heard of. It was in a more industrial part of town and the building looked like a real 1950s diner. Not one of the made over, brand-new-vintage kind, but a real honest to God diner that looked like the wiring would probably ignite at any moment and the ceiling tiles were made of asbestos. Shark liked it.

The place was small and had the red and white checked table cloths that he associated with food that would be as greasy as it was delicious. There was a light-up black Santa at the counter and the snowman painted in the window had dreads. He was the lightest-skinned person in the room and the guy behind the grill with the prison tatts on his knuckles gave him a serious look. Shark ignored him—he was used to that kind of attention. When Cerise came in shortly after he did and slid into the booth, the tension in the room palpably lessened. As always, he was a stranger in a strange land, only allowed in with a passport.

"Hey," said Cerise, flagging a waitress down. "Glad to see you got out of the whole being arrested thing."

"Thanks. It's easier when you actually didn't do it."

"Easier, but not necessarily easy," she said, with a wry tilt of her head.

"My lawyer wears Gucci and knows three-syllable words."

"Money does talk," she agreed. "Probably also helps that you're white-ish."

"Depends on who I'm standing next to. Too dark, not dark enough. Story of my life."

"Yeah, my cousin is bi-racial and bi-sexual," said Cerise, passing him a pile of printed sheets. "Basically, I get the impression that bi anything is tough."

Shark exhaled a surprised bark of laughter. "Well, at least I only have to worry about one of those."

After they ordered, he examined the papers she presented him with. "What am I looking at?"

"It's an email thread from Fowler's private account. I've highlighted what looks like the relevant portions. The basic gist is that Big Paulie used to take merch from Fowler and delivered it for him. But Big Paulie's sudden, uh, retirement caused a delay in delivery of the latest shipment and the buyers are very upset about it. Fowler doesn't want to be responsible for delivery because he thinks it puts him too much in the spotlight. But this Corbeau436 is putting a lot of pressure on him. "

Shark did not bother to point out that Big Paulie had technically died of a heart attack. No one ever believed him about that. "Who is the buyer?" he asked, skimming through the pages. "Who is Corbeau436?"

"Anonymous email account. I'm digging, but honestly, it could be months before I attach it to an actual human being."

"You know what's weird? 436 was my cell number."

"I have no appropriate response for that," said Cerise. "But Corbeau is French for raven or crow."

Shark grunted. That put a lock on it. This had to connect to the Scarecrow Jacks. He just wasn't sure how yet. There was a pause as his biscuits and gravy arrived and Cerise dug into her hash browns.

"That has got to be fried in lard. How are you getting anything vegetarian here?"

"Hush your mouth," said the waitress. "This is vegetarian." She waved her hand over the hash browns. Cerise nodded as if under a spell. "Vegetarian," she repeated.

"But—" began Shark.

"Vegetarian," said Cerise, thumping the table with her fork.

"Clearly vegetarian," said Shark. "Meanwhile, ma'am, if I could get extra bacon, that would be great."

"You bet," the waitress said with a wink.

"You always have to poke holes," said Cerise, annoyed.

"Yes," he agreed. "It's one of the reasons people don't like me."

Cerise snorted. "Only one of the reasons. I'm going back to working with just Peri. She has the decency to pretend not to notice these things."

"That's why she's better at being undercover than I am," said Shark, immersed again in the emails.

"It really doesn't bother you, does it? That Peri and I are women?"

"Right now, you two and Marko are the most professional

assets I have. I don't have the time or resources to worry about what's in your pants. I need talent. Fuck gender identity."

Cerise grinned. "You think about Peri's pants a little bit, though."

"None of your business," he said, setting his coffee cup down firmly.

Cerise smacked the bottom of the ketchup bottle. "She thinks about yours. I caught her checking out your ass."

"I'm not having this conversation," he said, which just made her laugh. "But speaking of Peri, any sign of child porn on Fowler's computer? Or anything in that direction?"

"No," said Cerise. "Which kind of surprised me. Peri's usually a deadeye about these things."

"She might still be right," he said, still reading. "Just means whatever he's doing isn't digital."

Cerise made an agreeing noise around a mouthful of hash browns.

"What's a *Gas Sandwich*?" he asked as his eyes landed on a highlighted portion of email.

"I'm not sure," she said. "I thought maybe some sort of drug slang? I thought maybe you would know."

"Doesn't ring a bell, but I stopped tracking that shit the second I stopped doing direct sales."

"The date and location, such as it is, are on page three or four."

He read, lifting up the sheets as his extra bacon and omelet arrived.

Alternate meeting proposal.

LOCATION: OVERPASS

DATE: 12/30

TIME: 0400

REQUIREMENTS: BUYERS TO PROVIDE ALL SECURITY& TRANSPORTATION

"I don't know what *overpass* means either," said Cerise.

"It's a road that goes over another road."

"Oh gee, thanks for explaining that. I meant, I don't know what it's code for."

Shark sighed. "I don't think it's code for anything. I think it's an overpass."

"Where?"

"I don't know," he said, "but I know someone who does."

"Well, lucky you," she said.

"Yeah," he said. "Real lucky."

After breakfast, he called Marko from the parking lot.

"You're up early," remarked Marko around a yawn.

"Yeah, I just talked to Cerise."

"What'd she get? Tell me we've got a location and a time."

"Sort of. We will once I talk to Peri, anyway. The question is: what do we do with the information?"

"Knee-jerk reaction? Jack that shit."

"What's the advantage? Aside from the fun of fucking his shit up. Why not just call in a tip to the feds or the cops?"

"We can't guarantee they'll follow up on it and even if they do, we can't guarantee that they can stick it on Fowler, or that Fowler will even be there. And even if they do arrest him, it could drag on for months. We need a crystal-clear case for the cops. We need this dickhead gone, like yesterday."

"I can get them to follow up on it," said Shark.

"You mean, your PO can make them follow up on it?"

"Yeah, that's what I mean. But you're right. Unless Fowler is driving, which from the emails is a definite no, tracing whatever it is back to him might be problematic."

"So we park it on his lawn. Let him explain that."

Shark laughed. "Or…" he stopped, struck by an idea.

"Or you've just come up with something brilliant?"

"Maybe. I'm not sure you'll like this one. We still have Big Paulie's storage unit, right?"

"Yeah, we just finished moving all that shit out of the bowling alley and into it yesterday morning. You said you didn't want to leave any possible contraband lying around."

"Yeah, we're going to need to empty it out again."

"Son of a bitch. Do you know how much they complained the first time?"

"Fuck them," said Shark.

"That's easy for you to say. You're not the one they complain to." Marko sighed. "OK, storage check. What else do we need?"

"We need a plan to jack that shit. Meet me at the bowling alley at about five and we'll see what we can come up with."

"Are you sure? We're open tonight."

Shark sighed. "Right. Because I'm an ex-con trying to make a go of it as a small businessman. Who knew pretending to go straight would be this much work?"

"Cost of doing business," said Marko.

"OK, let's meet at three before we open. Maybe I can get a hold of Peri before then. When does school let out?"

"Probably not before three," said Marko. "But, you know, she doesn't seem to attend a ton of school, so maybe if you ask nice she'll skip out. It probably depends on how last night went." Marko ended on a smothered cough that was a cover for a mixture of laughter and curiosity.

"Mind your own business," said Shark.

"I try, I try," said Marko, "but I'm supposed to look out for you. It's part of my job as your bodyguard."

"You know what? Fuck you. You're not my bodyguard. You're promoted. You're officially the number-two guy around here. Now, mind your own business."

Marko laughed. "Hey, you're the boss. Whatever you say. Anyone else you want me to bring in?"

"Top tier. Eddie, Beef, and Paper."

"Really, Paper? I mean, he's got a handle on the street-level shit. But creative planning is not his strong suit."

"I'm going to need some of the Blue Street crew on this gig and it would be rude to leave him out if we're using his guys. But tell him to bring Domingo along. That kid does have a brain and I need him to start getting some experience."

"Yeah, good call. Will do. See you at three."

Shark mulled over what to do about Peri. Any way he looked at things, she was not going to be happy. He wished that an unhappy Peri didn't matter to him, but it was undeniable that it did, and denying reality led to errors in judgment. He put off decisions in favor of a workout at the gym. One of the things he missed about prison was the enforced discipline of a daily routine. On the outside, it was too easy to let things slide.

After that, he finally worked up the courage to text her. Setting a time for what he was beginning to think of as their coffee shop. He hoped it escaped her notice that he'd set the meeting at a public location where she couldn't flip out. Not that she was the flipping-out type. More the direct and targeted violence type.

He had the feeling that no play was a good play with her. She wasn't going to like it if he worked an angle. How had he gotten himself in so deep? Still, he couldn't bring himself to regret the morning.

When she walked in to the coffee shop, he found himself smiling involuntarily. As usual she was wearing a messy braid on one side, and a few snowflakes had crystallized in the strands of her hair so that for a moment she sparkled.

He scooted the second chair around to his side of the table so she wouldn't have to sit with her back to the door. "I didn't order you anything. I didn't know what you would want."

She leaned in for a kiss, which he knew he shouldn't give, but did anyway.

"I'll order it," she said with a slightly guilty look. "I have a secret addiction," she said reading his expression. "Be right back."

When she returned, it was with the tiniest cup in the place.

He eyed the cup. "I have to know."

"Tiny sips," she said. He cautiously took a drink, then sat back as the sensation filled his mouth.

"Seriously, is there anything in this but chocolate?"

"Pretty sure there isn't. If you let it sit for a couple of hours it just hardens into a solid chunk."

He took another sip. There was a second flavor at the end of each sip, a heat like cayenne. It burned, but in a good way. "I can see why you're addicted. That's some dangerous stuff."

"It hits my caffeine need too. Chocolate has twelve milli-grams of caffeine to an ounce."

He laughed. "Because I can't be around to serve you cherry Cokes all the time?"

"Exactly! So what's up? Did you hear from Cerise?"

He liked that she always cut to the chase, but suddenly he was very nervous. "Um, yes." He reached in his jacket, pulled out the printouts of Fowler's emails and pushed them across the table. What if he was wrong?

She began to read. "No wonder he's been pushing you. If he doesn't deliver the merchandise it sounds like he's in deep shit. He set a sales date? What about location?"

He saw her grip tighten on the papers as she read on. When she reached the end she put them down, but didn't look at him. He practically could see her mind whirring through probabilities and possibilities. He waited nervously.

"You watched the video, didn't you?" she said finally looking him in the eye. "Otherwise, why would you know to bring this to me?"

He licked his lips. "Yes. I watched it last night. After all the effort to get the camera and card I was curious."

Her face was set. He'd seen this expression once before, right before she'd stabbed a guy.

"You know what? This is my fault," she said after a long moment. "I shouldn't have trusted you."

That brought him up short. He'd known he'd been in the wrong, but he hadn't put those words to it.

"No, that's not fair. I wasn't planning on using it for anything. I just wanted to know."

"And what if it had turned out to be some information that was useful to you? Oh wait...it did."

"I didn't need to tell you about this. There were at least two drug deals on the tape. Run the plates, find the drivers, and then I'll have the location. I'm actually trying really hard not to screw you over."

She took a sip of her chocolate-bar-in-a-cup, appearing to think about what he'd said. He hoped she believed him. He remembered the bitter sting of watching his girlfriend lie about him in court. He didn't need to give Peri that acid taste of disbelief. She had always been on the up and up with him. He didn't want to ruin that.

"And of course, if you tell me and I forgive you, then you don't have to go through the trouble of locating those dealers." Her face had softened slightly, but her sarcasm was still blistering.

"True," he agreed, digging in and going for broke. "And if you found out and I hadn't told you, I'm pretty sure sex would be off the table."

"Also true," she replied, hiding a smile behind her drink.

"But also, I don't know what you're working on at the overpass. I don't know what you're working on there, but I figured you might be interested in finding out more. Maybe if we roll up on Fowler, you will."

She looked amused and also pleased, as if he'd passed a test. "Why don't more people look at things from all the angles?"

"Maybe because they prefer to spare themselves short-term pain rather than looking at long-term benefits?"

"Probably. We are clear on the fact that snooping in my stuff is not cool?"

"Yes. Totally clear. Won't happen again. I swear." He raised his right hand. He would absolutely not do it again, unless he really had to. Peri looked unconvinced and he had a sudden irrational fear that she could somehow hear his thoughts.

"What do you think he's selling?" she asked.

"Not sure. Drugs or guns, most likely. Which will work out for me, because I can use it to incriminate him."

She was frowning. "What if it's something else? Something that you can't use?"

"Like what?" He had the feeling that she had something specific in mind.

She adjusted her braid self-consciously, rubbing behind her ear.

"I suppose it could be anything," said Shark. "Paper said whatever it is usually fits in boxes. I suppose it could be a dastardly fruit smuggling operation."

She ignored his joke. "Boxes. Yeah, you're probably right—guns or drugs." He wanted to ask what was bothering her, but she obviously didn't want to talk about it. He had to respect her limits. He already felt like he was getting away with a lot. "What's your plan?"

"Ah, the plan," he said. "Yeah, I don't think you're going to like it."

Shark: Rolling Thunder Lanes

"*That's* the plan?" Marko made a wide Italian gesture of general disbelief. "That is a terrible plan."

"I said you weren't going to like it," said Shark.

"Understatement of the year. Seriously, what's the first thing you learn?" Looking at the rest of the guys, he prompted, "That's not a rhetorical question."

"Never snitch," Domingo offered.

"Well, yes," admitted Marko. "But that's not what I meant."

"But is it really snitching, though, if you snitch on the cops?" mused Domingo.

"There are cops and there are criminals," Beef opined. "One should not pretend to be the other."

"All cops are dirty," said Paper. "This guy is just smarter than the rest of them."

"No," Eddie argued, "If you become a cop you're publicly stating that you follow the rules. Presenting yourself as a rule-follower and then taking advantage of other people's trust by breaking them is worse than being a straight-up criminal. The guy therefore deserves a worse punishment. If you break a primary rule, you cannot be protected by lesser rules. Gloves come off."

"But if we break a primary rule, then aren't we as bad as he is? Is that karmically sound?" Beef wondered.

"We're criminals. Our defining characteristic is that we break rules," Domingo said sagely.

"I blame this philosophical bullshit on you," said Marko, glaring at Shark. "The rule," he added loudly, as Shark smothered a laugh, "that I was referring to, was *don't wear a wire*. Nothing good can come from that. Even if everything goes smoothly and you don't get caught and killed, you'd still end up testifying."

"That would be boss," said Domingo. "What? It would be! Having the cops and lawyers all having to call him Mr. Santoyo and shit."

Shark tried not to smile at Domingo's obvious relish, but only half managed it. "In any case, I don't think I'll have to testify."

"If you wear a wire, you have to testify. Pretty sure that's how it works," said Beef.

"Well, I'm pretty sure I won't have to testify, because I'm *pretty sure* he'll get shanked in prison while he's awaiting trial."

"Oh," said Marko. "Yeah. We could make that happen."

"Look, we can argue about the what-if's until the sun comes up, but why don't we just assume that I can pull this off and move on?"

Marko threw up his hands. "I don't know why I'm arguing. You've done literally everything else you said you would do. I should shut my fat yap."

"OK, well, while Papa Bear shuts his fat yap, let's talk about phase one. The heist. From what Paper said about previous exchanges, the buyers brought their own truck, the merch was in unmarked boxes, and it was fairly heavy. Assuming this buy follows the pattern, we can expect one or two drivers in Fowler's truck." On a computer tablet, Shark opened the map. "This is the exchange location. It's tomorrow at two in the afternoon. That doesn't leave a lot of time to plan. I'm open to all suggestions. What have you got?"

"Get there first," suggested Eddie. "Wait until the truck stops, pop the driver, take the truck."

"Um," said Domingo. "What about the buyers? Without our people to shift the merch, won't the buyers bring extra guys to do the moving? What do we do about them?"

Shark had already had this thought, but he was glad to hear it coming from someone else. Eddie and Beef were also nodding their approval.

"Two teams," said Marko. "One takes out the buyers—if possible, before they get to the meet location—and the other takes Fowler's truck and the merchandise."

"Which one do you want?" asked Shark.

"The buyers, I guess," said Marko. "Is there a way we can figure out the route they're likely to take?"

"I'm going to talk to Cerise about hacking traffic cams," Shark said.

"That would be good. But we still won't have a lot of warning. And the closer to the meet location the better." Marko frowned at the map. "That's a pretty low-traffic area. I could do a simple block and stall. We *do* want to take them out?"

"Take them out," said Shark. "I'm not having fuckers run shit through our territory without permission. Doesn't have to be gruesome, but let's put the word out there. Leave the bodies, ditch the truck. Make sure there's nothing to tie it back to us."

Scrutinizing the map, Marko said, "This intersection would be ideal. I could use a couple of guys for a blocking accident, but it would sell more if I could use Peri." He cocked an eyebrow at Shark.

"We can ask. It is my impression that she doesn't do shoot-for-hire."

"I just need window dressing, to lure them out. But I want someone who won't panic."

"I'll ask. Who else do you want?"

"Eddie or Beef, and then a couple of the younger-looking guys from Paper's crew. Two cars for the accident and an SUV to block them in."

"My guys can get the cars," said Paper.

"Nothing too local," Marko warned.

"OK, that puts Paper and Domingo with me for the truck heist, with Marko taking out the buyers. Eddie, Beef, you guys got a preference?"

"Truck heist," they said in unison. Shark rolled his eyes as they proceeded through Rock, Paper, Scissors. Beef grinned when he won.

"Just make sure to tie up your damn hair," said Shark, pointing to Beef's three feet of locks. "And I don't mean a ponytail. Last time we had any action you nearly took an eye out with that thing."

"For reals," said Paper, who was the owner of the eye in question. "You should cut that shit."

"I can't. It's bad for my chakras," insisted Beef and they all groaned.

"You're white," scoffed Paper. "Seriously, I keep telling you—you got no chakras."

"Everyone does, regardless of race," said Beef. "Yours are always way out of alignment. If you would center yourself—"

There was another chorus of groans and Marko threw a French fry at him.

The doors opened and a couple of the gang-members-turned-employees strolled in.

Shark checked his watch. "Let's stop here for now and prep for opening. Marko and Eddie, why don't you drive out and scout your location. Beef and I will do ours tomorrow. I'll talk to our contractors and see if they're in. Paper, you'll work on the cars?"

"Yeah. Can I come on the location scout?"

Shark looked at Paper carefully. When he'd first arrived, Paper had done nothing but flex and give attitude. These days he had been a helpful soldier. Maybe there was hope for him yet. Either that or Paper was planning on shooting him in the back of the head. It could go either way.

"Yes," Shark said, "I think that's a good idea." Domingo looked hopeful but didn't say anything, and Shark gave him a nod. Domingo grinned.

The open sign had barely flashed on and Shark was still rummaging behind the bar trying to find the remote to find something besides the evening news on the bar TV when someone walked in. Shark gave him the once-over. Tall, white guy, short brown hair, unkempt beard, dressed in jeans and a heavy wool coat. Somewhere in his late thirties or early forties probably, but he looked fit. Shark watched the guy clock the exits and frown at poor Sarasota with the unfortunate neck tattoo as he carried a rack of glasses back to the kitchen. Not a cop, but definitely carrying, and he had the look of being serious trouble in a fight.

The man sat down at the bar as Shark switched to the sports channel.

"What can I get you?" He was behind the bar, might as well play bartender.

The man stared at Shark, and Shark waited. When it came to staring, he had his namesake's capacity to go without blinking for a very long time.

"I'll take a cherry Coke."

Peregrine: The Problem with Al

Drill team was on a water break when her phone rang. Peri frowned, but took the call. "Hey Al."

"Hey, where are you?"

"School. Drill team practice. Why?" She dug into her bag for a water bottle. They were rolling out mats onto the gym floor now and Peri watched nervously. The girls had been skeptical about adding Peri, and although she thought she was winning points on her physical fitness level, backflips were out of her league.

"I've been looking into that Fowler guy," said Al.

Peri took the phone up another few levels on the bleachers.

"I said *don't* look into Fowler. I said look into Happy Place," she said, furious, but trying to keep her voice down.

"Yeah, I looked into that. But I ended up looking into Fowler too. I've got something I think you need to see. When are you done?"

Peri considered that. That was a lot of effort for Al. It was as if he was actually trying to be helpful. She ought to reward that behavior. There was just one little hitch. "Well…"

"Well, what?" He sounded impatient.

"We were going to go bowling after practice."

"Bowling. Are you shitting me? Am I supposed to buy that?"

"Ashley has a crush on one of the guys who works at the alley and Madison says that the boys' track team is going tonight, so she wants to go." There was silence on the other end of the line. "Al?"

"Seriously, you're making this up, right?"

"Look, I joined the drill team to fulfill my PE credit and now I have social obligations. It's, like, a teenage expectation. I can't violate the expectation without getting ostracized."

"And your mom's OK with this?"

"Are you kidding? She's over the moon. She's all, *I'm so glad you're making new friends* and shit."

"OK, well, I'm over by the bowling alley now. When are you going to be here?"

"Not until like five or six depending on how long it takes Regan to do hair and make-up."

"Why do you keep saying this stuff? I do not want to know this shit. It makes my brain hurt."

"Al, women do hair and make-up. It takes a lot of effort to look effortless. You need to appreciate."

"You're all twelve or something. You shouldn't own make-up."

"Cleansing breaths, Uncle Al. You're going to have to come to terms with it sooner or later."

"It's going to be later. A lot later. Anyway, here's the problem. I've got a gig out of town and I'll be gone for a couple of days, but I think you need to see this shit. Where can I leave it?"

Peri sighed, weighing her options. "OK, if you're by the bowling alley, then you can leave it there. There's a guy, Domingo. He goes to my school. I helped his cousin out with a stalker situation last year. He'll hold stuff for me. Just ask for Domingo but for crying out loud, don't try and talk to him or anything. Last thing I need is for you to start talking to people I know."

"What's wrong with me talking to people?"

"Oh, I don't know. How about the fact that you freak them the fuck out? Remember poor Chelsea?"

"I was making small talk."

"You don't know how to make small talk. All you do is grill people. No wonder you can't get a date."

"I can get a date."

"OK, maybe a date, but not a girlfriend. I need to find you a nice CIA interrogator and see if you two can't settle down and make abrasive babies."

"Sounds hot. Anyway, I'll leave the envelope with Domingo. I'll call you when I get back into town. And don't go near Fowler."

"I told you, he's not my problem," she said. "Wouldn't go near that pervoid with a ten-foot pole. Also, don't die, I love you, etcetera."

"It's just out of town."

Peri rolled her eyes at the blatant euphemism that she wasn't supposed to know about. "Again: not twelve. I know out of town doesn't mean Kansas, Al. Just be careful."

"You too."

A few hours later Peri checked her reflection in the glass door of the bowling alley. She couldn't believe she'd let Regan do her make-up. It was a good look, but usually she applied cosmetics to become someone else. This was weird. It made her feel a little like a puppet of herself. It made her too visible. Although, if she was honest, she wanted to look good at least once for Shark. Every other time he saw her, she was dressed to look hideous. She wished she could just be visible for him and disappear for everyone else.

Domingo was working the shoe counter and it took forever to get him alone. Mostly because he was chatting up Ashley.

"Did someone give you an envelope for me?" she asked in the two-second break between when Ashley left the counter and when she returned to get different shoes.

"He talked to Shark. Not sure what he said, but Shark seemed kind of pissed."

"Son of a bitch! That man can never fucking follow directions. I said don't talk to anyone!"

"Shark's the boss. He does whatever the fuck he wants," said Domingo.

"I meant the other one. Where's Shark?"

"In the office."

There was more waiting around until she could plausibly take a bathroom break. She set the timer on her phone and went to find Shark. He was at the desk, shuffling papers around. She slid inside and started to close the door.

"Can't come in. I don't know who the cops have in here. When the alley is open, there's an open door, five-foot policy until after this Fowler thing is settled."

Peri tried not to feel that the new boundary was personal. She leaned against the doorframe. "Something was dropped off for me?"

"Yeah," he said pulling a manila envelope out from a desk drawer. "About that. I was not OK with that."

"Sorry," said Peri with a sigh. "He was supposed to give it to Domingo to hold, then leave." She took the envelope and flipped open her knife, preparing to slit the edge.

Shark's eyes sort of twitched. "It's not really about the mail."

What the fuck had Al done now? If he had fucked this up for her, she was going to make him pay. "OK," Peri said, making a soothing gesture somewhat undermined by the knife. "It was supposed to just be a drop-off. What happened?"

"The guy who stores your clothes came in, ordered a Coke, said he knew where I lived, and gave me an envelope."

Peri stared at Shark, unable to convert his words to actual sense. "Now when you say Coke, are you sure you don't mean bourbon?"

"He said he wanted a shot of bourbon, but that he also wanted a puppy, and then he ordered a cherry Coke."

Peri burst out laughing. "I knew it! I knew I could get him with the dog. I am so winning."

"I think you're missing the point," Shark said, his expression furious. "He said he knows where I live. I don't like being threatened."

Peri couldn't stop her head from tilting or her eyebrows from lifting. "And what did you say first?"

Shark's stare moved to a point above her head. Direct hit. He'd definitely said something first. He also looked like he was about to say several somethings to her.

"I know, I know," she said, slitting the envelope. "He's very upsetting. But he said it was about Fowler and I needed to see it." She tucked her knife away and dumped out the contents. It was a stack of photos. Fowler was in the first one, getting out of his car.

"He said you'd probably end up showing me anyway. How would he know that?" demanded Shark.

"Beats me. I haven't told him anything about you or Fowler, other than that he wasn't my problem." She sorted through the photos. "What can I say? Uncle Al is smart like that."

"Uncle Al," Shark repeated, then sighed and leaned against the door, breaking his own five-foot rule. "Peri...what?"

Peri handed him a photo. "We've got a problem."

He scrutinized the picture of Agent Fowler handing an envelope to their favorite Vagos—Mateo. "Son of a bitch. Where did your uncle get these pictures?"

"He's a PI. I told him to look into that Happy Place Youth Center that Fowler was pushing. This is what he came back with."

"A PI," echoed Shark. She couldn't tell if he was processing or pissed.

"Sam Spade? Hercule Poirot?" Staring. "Jim Rockford?" More staring. "Shawn Spencer and Burton Guster?"

"I know what a private investigator is. And I believe you mean Ghee Buttersnaps AKA The Heater, also known as Gus 'Sillypants' Jackson."

Peri laughed. "Exactly. Meanwhile, what do you want to do about this?" She tapped the picture in his hand.

"I want to think about it. We made a plan for Fowler's shipment. Marko wants you for window dressing. There would be gun play, but not by you. Do you want in? Cerise is on look-out via traffic cams. It'd be you, Marko, Eddie, and a couple of the others. Fake car accident."

"Distracted teen driver in a short skirt?" He nodded. "Usual rates?" He nodded again. "Sure. I am sorry about Uncle Al. He really was just supposed to drop shit with Domingo and go."

Shark sighed. "Do you think your uncle is likely to do anything unexpected before the shipment?"

"No, he's out of the country for a few days."

"OK, after he gets back, we'll figure something out."

She gave him a suspicious look, but her train of thought was interrupted by her phone's timer beeping. "And now we've reached the end of the allowable time that a girl can take in the bathroom without her friends coming to look for her."

He raised his hand as if he was intending to reach out, but he put it back down again.

"Five-foot rule. Right." She took a deep breath and let it out again. "I guess I'll just go be a cheerful girl over there in lane seven for a while."

"I'll call you tomorrow."

"Sure," she said, not turning back. "Need to discuss the thing with Marko."

"Peri," he said, and this time she looked over her shoulder. "You look really nice tonight."

She blushed. "My mom's staying in the city for New Year's Eve. You know, in case you don't have any plans."

"I don't have any plans," he said.

Shark: The Office

No. Shark tried mouthing the word.

It was not difficult. All he had to do was just say it.

"No, I can't see you anymore. No, I will not spend New Year's with you. No, I will not endanger my entire plan and deal with the FBI for a night with you."

He trusted Peri as much, if not more, than he trusted most people, but he wasn't about to blow up his life for her. Francesca de Corvo had taught him that much. What people said didn't matter. Their actions, that's what mattered. Francesca had promised him the moon and then she'd sent him to prison for a crime she'd committed. This morning's roll in the sheets had been a mistake—the visit from her uncle was enough to bring him to his senses on that one. It didn't matter that Peri could make him laugh. It didn't matter that he wanted her body in the worst way. It didn't matter that he needed her to get through this. And it didn't matter that it *felt* like he could trust her. The right answer was still *no.*

It would be a lot easier to say if she wouldn't smile at him.

Shark was banging his head against the desk when Marko came in.

"Problems?"

Shark sat back. "What is wrong with me?"

"You need a haircut."

"I was thinking of growing it out."

Marko looked pained. "Did you find out who the guy was?"

"Yeah, he's Peri's uncle."

"Whose side is he on?"

"At a guess, I'm going to go with Peri's."

"Well, that's all right then."

Shark pursed his lips. Peri's side was almost the same, but not exactly the same, as his side. He didn't feel like pointing that out. "This is what was in the envelope." He gave Marko the photo of Fowler and Mateo.

Marko took the photo and dropped into the other chair and put his feet up on the pressboard desk. Shark had thought about getting new furniture, but the office still looked a little tore up from when they'd moved in. Multiple people had searched it and he'd used a torch to cut the door off the safe in the floor. The shelves were a little crooked and Marko had hung a picture of a lighthouse over the hole in the wood paneling. New furniture would probably just point out how crappy everything looked.

"What the hell did you guys do to this Vagos?" demanded Marko.

"Nothing! Well, Peri accidentally sprayed him with gravel. But I mean…" Shark shrugged.

"You mean it's not like she stabbed him in the eye or anything? Right. Anyway, now Fowler is in with the Vagos? We should reach out to the Vagos. We've never had a beef with them. We might be able to head this off. Or at least find out if it's just this douchebag or the entire chapter."

"Well, considering he's the only Vagos I know in the area, I don't think I should be reaching out," said Shark.

"I'll ask the Fives. Do you want to cancel the heist?"

"No. Whatever Mateo and Fowler are doing, we can't miss this opportunity. We just have to hope they can't move fast enough."

"Is Peri in?"

"Yeah, and I heard from Cerise, so we've got a complete roster."

"I like Cerise, but I wish we had our own hacker," said Marko. "We could use someone who could do some of the processing on identity theft. It's annoying to have to outsource that shit."

"We don't use one enough for a permanent hire."

"But when we really need one, we really need one."

"True," agreed Shark.

"You talk to your PO yet?"

"Vivian's up next. Then Williamson."

Marko sighed. "What kind of crew are we running? We got the gay lawyer, the underage fixer, and the vegetarian hacker. I know this is the burbs, but jeez."

"If I had other solutions I would use them. And besides, we're getting the job done. You really going to complain about how the sausage gets made?"

"I am not complaining," said Marko holding up his hands. "And hey, you're right. So far we're batting a thousand. But I'm an old-school guy and sometimes I look around and think: what the fuck, how did I end up here?"

"How *did* you end up here?" Shark asked. "Why did Geier give you to me?"

Marko looked embarrassed. "I was doing bodyguard duty for him and one of the days at Kos, I bumped into his waitress. The damn steak went flying off the plate and landed right in front of him on the table. Yeah, go ahead and laugh. I thought I was going to die. I still wake up at night in a cold sweat over that. Anyway, you came in the next day and I was assigned to you."

"No wonder you never said shit! I thought you were the most discreet wise guy ever."

"I was just happy to not be dead. So thanks for coming back in, by the way. Saved my bacon."

"But not the steak," said Shark.

"Go fuck yourself," suggested Marko, rising. "On your other problems, which I assume to mean girl problems. My advice? Forget the PO. Stick with Peri."

"She comes with complications."

"Don't they all? But with Peri you don't have to lie about who you are."

If only that were true. For the first time, he wondered what Peri would think if she found out he was working for the FBI. Would she understand or would she hate his guts?

"Plus," continued Marko, "Peri will watch your back. The other one? I've seen her type before. She will fuck you up at the drop of a hat."

Friday ~ December 30

Peregrine: The Distraction

Peri sat on the hood of the stolen VW and stared at Eddie, waiting for the signal from Cerise. Eddie was Asian-American of some kind, but she'd never heard him specify. She supposed it didn't matter. His greater culture of influence was California, which is why he got along with Beef so well. They both dude-bro'd out periodically. For today's role, she had gone with a red, cotton stretch skirt that could be adjusted up or down over black tights. For the top, she'd gone with a gray and black bondage-inspired shirt with a lot of buckles and an asymmetrical zipper thing that could reveal quite a lot of bosom on demand and also hid her waist belt with knives. Winter sexy was hard to pull off unless she was willing to freeze her ass off, which she wasn't. Eddie had it easier with a leather jacket and jeans over boots.

"So," said Eddie, leaning against the other car. Peri waited. God knew what the leg-breaker was going to come up with for a conversation starter. "Domingo says you know about investing."

"Uh. Some. What did you want to know?"

"Well, there are some difficulties in our line of work. It's a cash business, but it seems like if I want to buy anything big everyone wants some sort of credit rating or something. And how am I supposed to get that? Everyone says you can't deposit too much cash. And what's the point of raking in the dough if can't actually buy anything?"

"Financial institutions are obligated to report cash deposits in excess of ten grand to the IRS. But you can tiptoe right up to that line. And if you employ a strategy of bank diversification you can dump a pretty good chunk into savings per year. I have the added complication of being under eighteen—they don't let you open an account without a guardian. But I've still got a couple of different retirement and college funds. Do you need a referral? One of my guys is used to people in your line of work. I mean, you can't say too much, you have to leave him plausible deniability, but he will work with you."

"Yeah, that'd be great!"

"I'll text you," she said, flipping through her contacts. Eddie read off his number and she hit send.

"So how many investing guys do you have?"

"A couple. I had to. I was carrying too much cash on hand. I mean, I'm a teenager, sooner or later my mom's going to have a freak out and search my room for drugs or birth control or some shit. And then I'm going to be stuck explaining why Winky Pegasus has ten grand and a pot brownie shoved up his ass."

"Right?" Eddie paused to review the last sentence. "I mean, I don't use a Pegasus, but I have similar problems. Between not being able to get ahead on anything and fucking Big Paulie, I was seriously thinking about going legit before Shark took over."

Peri was surprised. "Things were that bad?"

"Big Paulie and Zip… those dudes were assholes. I got into this because it was easy money and it seemed fun, not to put up with dipshits who couldn't pass the GED if they tried. Good thing Shark showed up when he did. I was gonna have to move and shit. Way not cool, man. Not looking forward to it."

"Shark does know how to put the fun back in crime," said Peri and Eddie rocked back on the car hood in silent laughter.

"So what *is* up with you—"

Both of their phones beeped, cutting off what was definitely going to be an awkward conversation.

Two minutes out.

Peri pulled off her coat and dropped it in the car. "How do you want to do this?" she asked, hiking up her skirt another three inches and unzipping her top down to cleavage level. "Should I just yell at you, or can I shove you?"

"Whatever is fine," said Eddie. "But I'm going to keep my gun side away from them. That means you'll have a better view when the action starts. If you could give me a clear signal when Marko makes his move."

"I'm just going to go with *now* and then I'm going to hit the deck. Good?"

"Cool. OK, let's do this."

"This is your fault, you dumbshit!" she shouted, gesturing widely. Eddie grinned.

"Don't smile at me! You think this is *funny?*"

A U-Haul truck rounded the corner and slowed as the driver saw Eddie, Peri, and the pair of cars they had placed across the roadway.

Peri carried on, screaming obscenities. Eddie did some yelling of his own and grabbed his crotch. The U-Haul came to a stop and sat idling while they went through a few more gyrations; Marko's SUV came around the corner and pulled up tight behind it, effectively blocking the truck from reversing.

The driver laid on the horn and Peri flipped him the double bird. There were three men in its cab. After another honk and Eddie shouting that the driver should engage in sexual congress with himself, finally, two men got out of the truck. Almost simultaneously Marko exited the SUV. Three of the Blue Street kids were dangling out of the SUV windows. Marko tapped on the driver's side of the truck. The driver rolled down the window.

The two from the truck had almost made their way up to Eddie. There was a bang as Marko pulled the truck driver out of the cab window and put a bullet in his head. Simultaneously, Peri yelled "Now!" and dropped to the ground. Above her she felt Eddie pivot and fire twice.

There was a rolling ball bearing sound as the back of the U-Haul slid up. Peri stayed down and tried not to listen to the sounds of yelling and gunfire. She saw Eddie's feet run past and heard Marko issuing commands to the kids from the SUV. Eventually, there was silence.

"Peri, we're clear!" Marko called and Peri got up, dusting road grit off of her hands. Aside from the three in the cab, there had been two in the back. The kids in the SUV seemed a little bit freaked, but the hands on their guns were steady. Marko looked pleased.

"Nice work everyone," said Marko, inspecting the corpses

closest to her. "Let's get the bodies loaded in the back of the truck. I'd like to point out Eddie and Peri's excellent signaling and partner work." From his shift in tone, Peri could tell he was moving into educational mode. She was pleased to see that the kids from the SUV were taking him seriously. "Also, please note Eddie's marksmanship—good solid center-mass hits. That's what you can achieve with practice. Now, as we discussed: Toto, you're taking the VW. Lawrence, take the Toyota. That leaves Peri and Griz in the SUV. Me and Eddie will handle disposing of the truck."

As Peri snapped on a pair of latex gloves and searched the pockets of the rapidly cooling bodies, Marko continued with his teaching moment. "This is also good. Peri has come prepared with gloves. Not only does that prevent her from leaving evidence, it also prevents her from catching anything from these meat bags."

Peri rifled through the wallets of the dead men. Two of the three were optimistically carrying condoms. They also had the usual assortment of driver's licenses, frequent-customer punchcards and credit cards, plus each had an unmarked key card. She laid out the contents on the pavement and snapped photos before shoving the contents back into the wallets. On impulse, she palmed one of the key cards before handing the wallets over to Marko.

"Remind them not to take credit cards?" she suggested.

"Ah, Peri makes an excellent point. As much as you would like to, don't take their credit cards, only the cash. It sucks to be popped for an identity theft that ties you right back to your perfect murder." He stripped the cash out of the wallets and doled it out to the boys.

"Speaking of cash," said Eddie, climbing out of the U-Haul's cab carrying a bra and a briefcase. "We've got the spoils of the job." He snapped the bra at one of the boys and then gave the briefcase to Marko, who flipped it open.

Peri retrieved the bra. It was a 32A—very small, as though for an adolescent.

Lawrence blinked. "That's a lot of cash."

"Yes, it is," said Marko. "Pop it in the back of the truck, Eddie. We'll bring it to Shark once we dispose of the truck."

Peri went to check the cargo space. Empty. Once again, she had come up with nothing.

"All right, gentleman and lady," Marko said, wiping his hands off on a handkerchief, "again, nice job. I'll see you all back at the bowling alley in an hour."

Peri got in the passenger seat and Griz, her assigned driver, got in beside her. "We're going to the chop shop first. Is that cool?" he asked quietly.

"No problem." Peri said and zipped her top back up.

Griz didn't speak again until they got to the chop shop and, even then, it was only to the guys at the door. She hung around, looking at the photos she'd taken of the wallets and waiting for Griz to return. She knew she was getting looks from the grease monkeys, but she didn't bother to look up and confirm their attention.

A purple Honda was being driven into the yard. "Got a new car," said Griz.

"Hot," she said, because something seemed to be expected of her.

"Yeah," Griz sighed.

They were halfway back to the bowling alley when her phone began to light up with texts. Griz was being a careful driver, obeying the speed limit and he pulled up at a stoplight in as slow idle as she checked her phone.

911.

Bowling Alley.

Now.

911.

She held out the phone for Griz to see. "From Paper."

He didn't wait for the light to turn green—the car accelerated in an instant, tires squealing as they took a turn and blew past a mini-van with a disapproving mom behind the wheel.

Peri got out of the Honda just as Marko pulled up.

"Nine one one's?" he demanded, slamming the car door and heading for the bowling alley in long strides.

"From Paper," said Peri, hurrying to match him. "What's going on?"

Marko shook his head. "I tried to call Shark. I didn't get an answer."

Peri felt a constricting in her chest.

The bowling alley was a mess. Bloody towels littered the floor around Domingo, who sat in a chair, shirtless and clutching a bottle of tequila. Beef, his hair in a topknot, was stitching up a wide gash in his side.

Paper paced back and forth, phone in one hand and a cigarette in the other.

"You're here," Paper gasped, relief sweeping his face. Shark was nowhere to be seen. Peri's hands felt clammy.

"What happened?" demanded Marko, his voice filling out with bass, like it did when he wanted everyone to pay attention. "Where's Shark?"

Paper gaped at them and swallowed hard. "We got the merchandise. Everything was going fine." He seemed unable to continue.

"Where is Shark?" Peri demanded.

"Gone," Paper whispered.

Peri punched him. She didn't mean to. It was like her arm acted on its own. Paper stumbled back and fell.

"They took him," he gasped from the floor. "And he'd said we had to stick to the plan. Always stick to the plan. So, we took the merch and came back here! That was the plan!" He was babbling.

Peri stopped and took a breath. *Took him* was not the same as dead. She could feel Marko looming behind her. Peri waved him off and grabbed Paper by the shoulder. "I'm sorry," she said with a fake smile, hauling him to his feet and pushing him into a chair. "I sometimes have a reflex reaction to bad news. Let's start again. You went on the job. You got the truck?"

Paper nodded. "We dumped the driver and his partner. It was going fine and then the Vagos showed up."

"You're sure it was the Vagos?" asked Marko.

"They weren't wearing their colors, but I recognized a few of them," said Beef. "It was definitely them."

"They tried to take the merch," continued Paper. "We fought. I got the truck rolling. Shark was in the back with Domingo, but when I looked back, he was on the ground with a gun pointed at his head."

"Was he dead?" asked Peri.

"No," slurred Domingo. "This guy… this guy was gonna gut me." There was a second delay while Domingo tried to focus. "But Shark tackled him out the back, right as the truck took off. I saw him move, but the Vagos didn't shoot. I saw him kick Shark, but he didn't pull the trigger. Shark was alive when we left."

Peri found one of the photos from Al in her bag and shoved it in Domingo's face. "The Vagos you saw—was one of them this guy?"

Domingo squinted. He was sweating and he groaned as Beef tied off the stitches. "Yeah. I think so. His hair was down, but I think so."

Peri's knees felt a little wobbly as she heard the news, but she tried not to show it.

"What do you think?" Marko asked her. "Will they have killed him?"

"No. That's Mateo. He knows Shark. And he'll know what he's worth, at least to me. They'll take him back to the clubhouse and then they'll offer to trade him for the merchandise."

"We can't lose the merch," said Marko, "or the plan is fucked."

"Yeah, well, we can't lose Shark or the plan is fucked," argued Beef.

"We'll offer them the cash from the buyers," said Peri.

"You think they'll go for it?" asked Marko

"It's a good bet," said Beef. "I don't think they'll have any loyalty to this ATF prick."

Marko nodded. "Ok, then why haven't they contacted us?"

Peri checked her phone. "It's forty minutes from the site to the clubhouse. That means they probably just got there. They'll probably call soon. Which means, if we mobilize now, we have a window of opportunity."

"To do what?" demanded Paper, panic coloring his tone.

"Save Shark's life," replied Peri. "Now, which one of you can use a rifle?"

Shark: Vagos

Shark laid down a suite of twos and tried to hold out hope that the day would only end with him getting his ass kicked at Gin Rummy. He couldn't be mad at his crew. He kept telling them to stick to the fucking plan. He just wished they'd stuck to it while he'd still been in the truck. He hoped Domingo was still alive. That gash in his side had been gushing blood when Shark had tackled the Vagos out of the truck and onto the pavement. Domingo's frightened face in the back of the truck was the last thing he'd seen before Mateo had kicked him in the head. From the sharp pangs in his ribs, that wasn't the only place Mateo had kicked him.

Shark felt like an idiot. His only hope was that Marko would make a deal for him. But would he? If Shark accidentally and unfortunately died, Marko would step in as territory boss. Marko felt like a friend, but friendship didn't run very deep in The Organization. He looked around the room, trying to estimate his chances of getting out alive.

The Vagos had set their clubhouse up in an old roadside bar. The pool tables had seen better days, but the bar was still functional. One of the members was even serving as a bartender. Besides El Perro, there were at least twenty guys in the room—all carrying.

The odds were not in his favor.

El Perro picked up Shark's discard and laid down four kings. Shark frowned. His grandmother would have tapped him upside the head by now. Aleja Santoyo had always said that if you couldn't focus on the game then you shouldn't play.

One of the men came in and whispered in El Perro's ear. It had been a long time since Shark had been able to slip seamlessly between English and Spanish, and the Mexican accent was throwing him, but he wasn't that impaired. Gleaning that a deal had been struck, he felt a wave of relief.

"Your people want you back," said El Perro. There was just a hint of an implication that he was surprised.

Shark laid down three queens. "I'm fun at parties."

El Perro snorted a half-laugh, then he scooped up the discard and laid down all of his cards. "Gin," he said. Shark tried not to get irked. He really had been good at this game once upon a time.

"What if we just killed him?" suggested Mateo from the bar. Mateo was a slick-looking man. Hair pulled back into a ponytail, no scars, nose showed a little damage from a previous break, but that was all. In Shark's opinion, he was too pretty to be a Vagos. "Whoever they send," continued Mateo. "We could just take the money and kill them both."

"Because *that* won't start a war," Shark said.

El Perro shot him a look, but it was clear that he was trying not to be amused. "We stick to the plan."

Shark won the next hand and was feeling slightly better

about his skills when he heard the crackle of the radio on the man stationed by the door. The contact had arrived.

Shark expected to see Marko's reassuringly burly form. Instead Peregrine Hays walked in, carrying a briefcase.

Why?

Why would she be here? This was a bad proposition for her. Best-case scenario led to barely getting out alive. What was the angle? He forced himself to sit perfectly still as his brain whipped through a maze of competing motivations and possible reasons trying to find a way that this made sense for her. His thoughts dead ended when he realized that there was only one reason for her to be here.

She had come for him.

Every instinct wanted him to push over the table and go get her, but some instincts should be ignored. She planned for everything—she must have a plan for this.

She was wearing a red miniskirt over black tights and a black shirt under a leather jacket. She looked sexy as hell and Shark guessed that it was her *distracted teen driver* costume. It was also working to distract every man in the room. She scanned the room with an unimpressed look and took a few steps in. He saw her clock Mateo at the bar, but behaved as if she hadn't noticed.

Mateo tossed down a shot of whiskey and stepped out in front of her.

"You can give that to me," he said, beckoning at the briefcase. He parted his jacket to expose the revolver shoved into the front of his pants.

The room was watching. Most situations, Shark had found,

had a pivotal moment—a moment that dictated everything that followed. This was it.

Shark watched as Peri leaned toward Mateo and delicately sniffed the air around him. "I only deal with the boss. You don't smell like the boss. You smell kind of pretty. Like a bitch."

Shark flicked his eyes to El Perro—for a moment El Perro's face registered amusement, but it was immediately wiped away.

"How about I show you who the boss is?" Mateo growled, looming over her, obscuring Shark's view of her. Under the table Shark's hands clenched into fists.

Peri's hand shot out and she put her hand on the pistol but she didn't pull it free of Mateo's waistband.

"And how about I pull the trigger?" Peri asked, pulling back the hammer on Mateo's gun, with a metallic click. Mateo's spine stiffened, but wisely he made no other movement. Neither did anyone else. "Now personally, I don't enjoy being this close to your dick, so why don't you back up—slowly—and let me talk to the boss."

Mateo did as he was told. She kept the gun, sliding it out of his pants. Shark could see that Mateo wanted very badly to kill her now. Earlier he had only wanted to make her lose and put Shark down, but now he wanted them both dead. That was going to be a problem.

"That was our heist," said El Perro. He put down a set of threes and lifted a finger, waving Mateo aside. Mateo moved back to the bar. "I want my merchandise."

"It's not coming," said Peri. "I brought the cash value

instead." She plunked the briefcase onto an empty table and put the gun down next to it. The tension in the room relaxed slightly.

"Those weren't the instructions," El Perro said, fixing her with a hard stare.

Peri stared back. "Did you follow *your* instructions?"

Shark realized he was holding his breath. It was a good play—an aggressive question, but intriguing enough that El Perro would have to follow up.

"Excuse me?"

Peri opened her coat—the movement was way too fast, and Shark distinctly heard three different clicks as guns were cocked. Slowing her movements, she took the envelope from the inside pocket and tossed it onto the table in front of El Perro, careful not to hit any playing cards. Messing up someone's game in progress was just rude, and she was nothing if not considerate.

"Open it," El Perro told Shark.

Shark's eyes flicked to hers and she gave a nod. With a shrug, he complied, and on top of the discard pile he laid out the photos of Mateo accepting the payoff from Fowler.

"Whose idea was it to hit the shipment?" asked Peri.

"None of your business," El Perro said.

"I'm just saying that prior to this incident we had a nice little system where we all ignored each other. I didn't mess with Vagos shit. Vagos didn't mess with The Organization, and they didn't mess with my…" Peri hesitated, picking the right word, "friends. So what changed?"

Shark made a mental note to ask later about the previous

arrangement. If they made it to later. They were also going to have to pick a better description than *friend*.

El Perro rolled his neck, cracking vertebrae loudly.

"In case you don't know," said Shark. "That guy paying off Mateo is ATF Agent Larry Fowler."

The attention of the bar rested on Mateo.

Mateo took another hasty gulp of whiskey. "It's not what it looks like. He wanted me to pop Shark, and I figured sure, but why not take Fowler's shit at the same time?"

"And when it went bad, you figured you would trade Shark for the merchandise and kill him anyway?" supplied El Perro. "You thought you could keep everyone happy?"

"Well…"

El Perro stared at Mateo.

This wasn't the first time that Mateo had ratted someone out. Mateo had been in lock-up at the same time as Shark. It had been his habit to find out about everyone's dirt and then rat them out when it became convenient or amusing to him. Shark guessed that up until now, that little habit hadn't affected El Perro.

"You present me with a problem," El Perro announced, turning to Peri. "I can't just let the two of you walk out of here. Actions must have consequences."

Peri was quiet for a moment. There was a double meaning in El Perro's words. Mateo was indeed a problem for him—serving two masters could not be allowed. But starting a war with Shark's people was also a problem. Shark knew what he would do in her position, but he had no idea if that was her plan. He just hoped that no one could see him sweat. He didn't want to embarrass Peri. She looked as relaxed as if this were the lunch hour at her high school.

Peri looked at Mateo as if sizing him up. "I'm in the business of providing solutions. I'll tell you what. I'll fight Mateo for it."

The room erupted in laughter. Shark sat back in his chair. He knew El Perro was watching him. He tried not to give anything away as he went over the factors. Could she make this work? She was good, but how good? Did she have a back-up plan? Mateo had been drinking, but if he really got his hands on her, she'd be in trouble.

"If I win, Shark and I walk out of here—we keep the merch and the cash. He wins… Well, you've got the cash and you'll still have Shark."

El Perro seemed to give it some thought. It was a stall. Shark had never wanted telepathy so much in his life. She had to know it was a stall. The bartender was handing Mateo something, but she didn't turn her head. She was watching El Perro as if waiting for the starting gun.

"OK," El Perro said, and Mateo charged. He had the bartender's gift—an enormous Bowie knife—in his hand.

Shark took a deep breath as Peri's left hand flicked out her first knife. She ducked down low, side-stepping under one meaty paw. She swiped the blade across Mateo's chest. Shark heard the transition as it slid from Mateo's leather jacket to flesh. Mateo spun away, as she flicked out the second knife with her right hand, dropping the handle, transitioning it to an against-the-arm hold. Shark wasn't sure that Mateo had seen the movement of the second knife opening. He hoped not. She feinted with the left, charging in, keeping the right hand tucked back. Mateo sucked in, stepping back slightly and Shark saw him grin as he avoided the cut.

Mateo swung in and she blocked with her right arm. Mateo realized his error as the full weight of his arm crushed in against the hidden blade. His knife went skittering out of his hand.

Blood dripped from his wrist as he charged back in and she swept upward along his torso with the right hand, cutting deep. He staggered, but he pressed forward, smothering her next strike. His hands closed around her neck, and Shark tensed in his chair, preparing to make a move. El Perro put his revolver on the table and gave Shark a look, but no one else moved.

Peri didn't look scared. She looked determined. She brought her left elbow down on Mateo's forearm. The impact pushed his arm a few inches down her chest and cleared room for her to jam the knife in her left hand into his throat. Shark heard the inhale of breath around the room and he scanned looking for further reaction. Still no one moved. Mateo had zero friends in the room. There was a crunch as she pierced the throat and pushed harder, looking for the brain. Then she switched the hold on her right hand and slid the point in between his ribs, puncturing the heart.

Shark watched the light in Mateo's eyes die. Peri staggered slightly as Mateo's weight collapsed onto her. She pushed him off and pulled her knives free as the body slid to the floor.

The room was silent.

Shark felt a deep desire to jump out of his chair and flip

them all the bird. That was his girl. And she was the fucking baddest bitch in the place. In any place.

Peri leaned down and pulled the bandanna out of Mateo's back pocket and cleaned her knives with it.

She was so fucking hot.

El Perro walked over to her she ignored him. Shark felt his gut clench. This was it. They were either going to die here or El Perro was going to stick to the deal. But there were worse ways to go out—at least he'd go out with someone who had his back.

"Did you decide to kill him before you got here or after?" he asked, nudging Mateo's body with his boot.

"After," said Peri, closing her knives and tucking them away. "I like to keep an open mind. And now if you don't mind, I'll take what's mine."

She finally made eye contact with Shark and he grinned. Yeah, fair enough. He was hers. She could claim him all she wanted.

El Perro gestured at Shark. Straightening his jacket, he stood up and put his sunglasses on.

"The money stays," El Perro announced.

"That wasn't the deal," Peri said. Shark watched her, waiting for a signal. This was her show.

"You want things to return to the previous system?" asked El Perro. "The pleasant system where we all pretend each other do not exist? Then the money stays."

"I don't like paying ransom," said Peri. Behind his sunglasses, Shark felt his eye twitch. She always had to argue. "There's no guarantee I won't have to pay again."

"It's not ransom. It's debt collection for Durrville." El Perro's face wore a faint smile.

Peri blushed. "The money stays, then it's debt paid?"

"Debt paid," agreed El Perro and held out his hand. Peri shook it. "Nice to finally meet you."

"You too," Peri said. "And now if you'll excuse me, I have other people to kill today." Shark knew she was aiming for funny, but he could tell that no one else was taking it that way.

"Of course," said El Perro, "*La halconita*, she is always flying. The ATF Agent, I assume?" Peri nodded and he smiled. "Good hunting."

She turned to Shark. "Ready to go?"

"Whenever you are."

"*Eres un hombre afortunado*," remarked El Perro.

Shark laughed because truer words had never been spoken. "*Lo sé*," he replied, and shut the door behind them.

"Keep walking," muttered Peri once they were outside. He grabbed her hand. "Marko has eyes on us from the field. Paper will pick us up."

They had barely reached the end of the gravel parking lot when Paper pulled up in Marko's boat-sized Mercedes. Peri got in first, sliding across the bench seat to make room for Shark. Paper handed Shark a pistol and then peeled out, spitting gravel. He wanted to slide across the seat and kiss her, but Peri and Paper were both focused on the Vagos clubhouse behind them, which was probably smart.

They rounded a bend and pulled up on a turn-out. Marko appeared, jogging across the field, his white clothes blending in with the snow-covered stubble in the field. The only thing truly visible was the black case that carried his rifle. No one spoke as Marko put it in the trunk and then got into the passenger seat. Marko clicked his seat belt shut as Paper pulled back onto the road. It made Shark feel better that Peri hadn't been as alone as she'd appeared.

"It went good?" asked Marko, glancing at Shark and Peri's clasped hands. Hers were still sticky with blood.

"Yeah, it went great," said Shark and then turned to Peri. "What happened in Durrville?"

Again, embarrassment crossed her face. "I accidentally blew up a couple of their bikes."

"Accidentally?" Marko echoed, making air quotes.

"Hey, shit happens. I can't control for all factors," Peri said defensively. "I didn't know they were going to be there, and I didn't think they could link it back to me. I guess I was wrong. Shark, What did El Perro say as we were leaving?"

"He said I was a lucky man."

By the time they reached the bowling alley he could tell Peri was starting to come down. She looked pale, he could tell that she wasn't tracking the conversations around her, and her hand in his was on the shaky side. It was a totally normal reaction to a high stress situation. If the world were perfect he'd be able to take her home and spend the rest of the day helping her work off the excess adrenaline. Sadly, today was a fucking nightmare.

In his absence, nothing had moved forward on the original plan and he knew they were going to have to haul ass to get back on schedule. The gang was scrambling to obey his orders when he was finally able to take a break. "Marko, I'm taking Peri home. I'll be back. Try not to let any shit blow up while I'm gone."

"You got it, boss. Try not to get kidnapped while you're out there. We're out of petty cash."

Shark laughed. "Got it. Back in a little bit." He led Peri to the exit, and put her in his car. She put up no resistance, looking blank

"Do you want me to take you home?"

She blinked at him and then smiled ruefully. "Sorry. I'm coming off the adrenaline. I'm getting kind of foggy. No, don't take me home. Take me to Al's. I'll shower off and catch a Lyft home."

"I'll wait and drive you."

She shook her head. "You've got a lot to get done. You should've had Marko drive me."

"Yeah, right. That's what I'm going to do."

She smiled.

Al's Bronco was still absent from its parking spot when Shark walked her to the door. "I can't believe you did that," he said.

"Well, what was I supposed to do?" Her hand snuck out and grasped his shirt.

"Let me die?" he suggested.

"I wouldn't do that." She looked horrified and the hand on his shirt twisted tightly.

"I know," he said, because he did. He could count on her in a way that he'd never counted on anyone.

"You're going to get ick all over you," she protested as he leaned in to kiss her.

"I've got a spare shirt in the car." He wrapped his arms around her. She stopped resisting and kissed him back. She felt tiny and delicate and smelled like sweat, flowers and blood.

When they finally came up for air, they stood with their foreheads resting against each other.

"Peregrine Hays," he said, kissing her softly, "I don't have the words to describe you."

She sighed and kissed him again, her fingers caressing his jaw and sliding into his hair. He loved the sensation as she stirred the hairs along the back of his neck. "You don't have time for this," she said, holding on to him.

"God, I wish I did." He took a deep breath and stepped away. "Tomorrow, I won't be able to call you. Even after everything is all over. I'll probably have to fill out paperwork and make statements and then I might have to take a trip into the city."

"I know." Her voice was flat. "But will you at least text? I want to know you're OK."

"Yes. We're still on for tomorrow night though, right?"

"Yes," she said. Her smile was sweet and a little bit shy.

He backed away from her, grinning. "I told you New Year's was going to be better."

Shark: The U-Store It

At the U-Store It facility, Shark put on the spare shirt he kept in the trunk.

"Hey," said Shark pulling on the shirt as he walked over to Marko, who was watching the crew unload the final boxes from Fowler's truck.

"You OK?" asked Marko frowning at him.

"Yeah, why?"

Marko lifted Shark's shirt up "Because I'm pretty sure that's a boot print."

Shark looked down at his ribs, where the imprint of someone's size ten could be seen. "Yeah, that'd be from Mateo. I've had worse from Geier, though, and he *likes* me. Plus, you know Mateo's not going to be doing it again, so that problem is solved."

"Peri sure sliced the shit out of that guy," said Marko, with an approving nod.

"How did you have any sight lines in there? The windows were all blacked out."

"Infrared scope," Marko said. "She had a set of LED lights in her jacket. If shit went south she was going to flash them at me and I'd start blasting."

"Smart," said Shark. "Thanks, by the way. For coming to get me."

"What was I going to do? If you die, then I have to take over. And I can't fucking do the accounting." Shark laughed. "Hey, before we head out can you go talk to Domingo and Paper? They're kind of freaking out. They think you're mad at them for ditching out on you."

Shark rolled his eyes. "Yeah, all right. Where are they?"

"Domingo's in the back of Paper's Honda."

Shark nodded and went to Paper's neon green rice-burner. He opened the back door and knelt down to look in at Domingo. "How are you doing?" he asked, scrutinizing the teenager. Domingo looked pale, but better than he'd been expecting.

"I'm OK." He assured Shark, waves of tequila rolling off him.

"Yeah, you are," said Shark. He took the bottle away, eyeballing the stitches. Paper and Beef peered into the back seat from the other side of the car and Shark handed the bottle to them. Then he went back to looking at the slice along Domingo's flank. "Well, one thing's for sure—I will not be using Beef for my tailoring."

"Hey, my pants always look great," objected Beef. "If you don't mind one leg being three inches shorter."

Shark chuckled. "You're taking him home?" he asked Paper.

"His moms works two jobs and I don't want him home with the boyfriend. I'm going to take him to my place where the guys can look after him."

Shark nodded. That was probably for the best. "No more booze. Lots of water. Keep the wound clean. Change the bandage at least once a day."

Paper nodded.

"I'm sorry," said Domingo, grabbing his arm.

"For what?" Shark asked. Domingo didn't seem to be able to form a sentence.

"Shit went sideways there," Paper supplied, stepping up for his boy. "It was my fault. I shouldn't have taken off or at least I should've checked the rearview. I'm the one who screwed up."

"Shit went sideways, but not because of anything you guys did," Shark told them. "If anything, I should have seen it coming. Everyone did their job."

Paper blinked at him. "You said stick to the plan."

"Right. And you did that. You stuck to the plan and we all made it out alive. That's what counts." He patted Domingo's shoulder. "Now let's get this done, so we can all go home and get as drunk as Domingo."

Paper and Beef laughed. He looked over his shoulder, hearing Marko yell for him. "Back in a bit."

"I really thought he'd hit me," said Domingo, as Shark walked away.

"I don't think he works that way," Beef said. "I think his chakra is too centered for that."

Shark almost turned around, but instead he kept walking. Maybe they were right. If he was the person he was pretending to be, he probably should have worked them over a bit. For the chakra comment if nothing else. Geier would have. But wasn't that why he was doing this—to *not* be like Geier? If this was his crew, then he was going to run it his way. They hadn't done anything wrong.

He ducked into the facility and went down the hall. Marko was waiting for him at the storage unit.

"Where we at?" he asked Marko. "Can I call Williamson yet?"

Marko shook his head. "Slight problem. Something you need to see." He slid open the door to Big Paulie's storage unit. Inside, the guys, wearing gloves, were unpacking guns out of the boxes from Fowler's truck and laying them out on the shelves. "Notice anything about these pieces?"

Then Shark saw it. They all had little labels zip-tied to them. "They're all tagged as evidence."

"Right. And then there's this." Marko went to three boxes stacked in the center and yanked open the one on top.

"Let me guess, they're full of Geier's drugs?"

Marko tilted the box to show Shark the contents—bag after bag of white powder marked with red diamonds.

"How'd you know?"

"Gas Sandwich," said Shark.

"What?"

"Geier keeps a tight hold on his supply line, the only place that mass quantity went missing was to the Feds. He paid a guy in the evidence lock-up named Fardisburger to confirm everything was still there. But come on… if the only place quantity has gone missing is to them, then maybe you shouldn't just be taking his word for it. Maybe you should be looking into who else is paying Fart Burger. The part that made me certain was in Fowler's emails. There was a reference to getting more from the Gas Sandwich. It's not the most original alias."

Marko grinned. "Crease is going to be so fucking pissed."

"Tell me about it. Meanwhile, let's move those boxes back to the bowling alley. No reason to give sellable, useful shit back to the cops. Take one of the boxes and distribute it to our guys. Tell them we want the usual cut, but they don't have to make the direct purchase. Call it a Christmas bonus. The other two we'll take back to Geier."

"Fuck, I love you," said Marko.

"I thought you said we weren't that open."

"I'm changing my mind," said Marko. "Results don't lie."

"This is the last box," Eddie said as he came in. "Did we decide what to do about the boxes of diamonds?"

"They're all going back to the bowling alley. One box gets distributed. Tell Paper to make a list of his guys that deserve a bonus," said Marko. "The rest go back to Geier."

Eddie looked to Shark and he made a Marko kind of gesture that Shark couldn't interpret. "I swear to fucking God I was thinking about getting a job as a personal trainer with my cousin at his gym."

Shark looked to Marko for an explanation. "Job satisfaction is up?" suggested Marko as Eddie grabbed the box of diamonds.

"Fuck yeah, dude, job satisfaction is way up," Eddie said and left whistling.

"Well," said Marko, "I guess everyone likes your management style. Meanwhile, I think we'll be out of your hair in about five minutes. You're clear to call Williamson. You really want us to wait at the bowling alley? I don't like leaving you here without back-up. I wish you had Peri or something. I'd be a lot happier."

"Wouldn't we both. But come on, I'll have cops backing me up. They may not be Peri, but they can't suck that bad."

"We'll find out," Marko said. "Good luck."

Shark dialed Williamson as the boys pulled away. "Hey, it's me. How's the deal with the cops going?"

"We have an agreement," Williamson said. "As you guessed, they want you to wear a wire."

"That's fine. Tell them to meet me at the U-Store It on fifty-first in an hour. Fowler is going to meet me here at three. You come too."

"That's a fast turn-around. They aren't going to like it."

"He's pushing me. If I delay, he'll get suspicious."

"I'll see what I can do," said Williamson.

Next he dialed Fowler.

"Funny story," Shark said when Fowler picked up. "I was driving along and there was this truck with all these stolen guns in it. Every single one of them marked as evidence. And now I've got them sitting in a storage unit. What do you think I should do with them?"

"Fuck you."

"It didn't have to be this way," Shark said. "You should have just offered me a cut. We could have handled our business without all this bad blood."

"You are going to die!" Fowler yelled.

"Really? And who is going to do the job? Mateo and the Vagos? Yeah… maybe you missed the news flash: Mateo had to take a long, permanent vacation."

Shark could hear Fowler breathing heavily. "Here's what's

going to happen," he continued. "You're going to buy your merch back from me—same price you were getting from Scarecrow Jack's crew. You're going to meet me in three hours with the money. I'll call you in two and a half hours with the location. Bring a truck. I had to get rid of yours."

"You're going to pay for this."

"No. You are. You have two and a half hours to get the cash together."

He tried Vivian next. She didn't pick up. So much for the full support of the FBI.

Williamson arrived first. Then the cops.

The wire was ridiculously large. He wondered how anyone managed to get anything recorded. How did snitches not get caught on day one? Where were all the James Bond spy-cams? Not in suburban America apparently.

The detective in charge was named Freedman. He was a tall, lanky black guy with a poker-worthy resting expression. As they were taping the wire to Shark's chest, he asked if they'd heard from Vivian.

"I called her," said Freedman. "We're going to have to go without her."

"Guess so," said Shark, feeling annoyed. The least she could do was show up and act like his Parole Officer.

The tech guys had wired up his phone. Under Freedman's watch, he dialed Fowler again.

"Where?" demanded Fowler, dispensing with all formalities.

"The U-Store It on fifty-first. Unit 178. Be there in thirty minutes."

Fowler hung up.

"OK," Freedman said. "Remember, we don't even have security cameras inside the building, so you have to get him on tape."

Shark was fairly certain that the entire reason that Big Paulie had selected this storage facility was that there were no security cameras.

"Fowler's statements have to be clear or we don't have anything," continued Freedman. "Otherwise, it'll just be your word against his that Big Paulie was buying illegal arms from him."

"I understand."

"Your emergency phrase is *party time*. Say that and we'll move in. But hopefully everything just goes well. Then you complete the sale and we'll bust him when he comes out. Do you understand?"

Freedman turned away and Williamson stepped forward clutching a frothy coffee drink. "I think I'm more nervous than you are. How are you this calm? What if this guy shoots you?"

Shark shrugged. "Then I'll probably die."

"Remind me never to ask you to cheer me up."

Shark grinned. "But if I do die, could you please sue the shit out of them?"

"Down to their last dime," said Williamson seriously.

Shark walked over to unit 178 and waited. He wasn't wearing an earpiece. It had been deemed too obvious. All he had was his phone. He checked the time again and bounced a little on the balls of his feet, wishing he could have run a warm-up lap like a boxer. His phone beeped with an incoming text from Williamson.

He has Vivian Flood. Plan screwed. They're scared to lose hostage.

Shark's adrenaline spiked and for a moment he considered running to the front of the building and just shooting Fowler as he entered. Instead, he forced himself to lean back against the wall.

Fowler appeared shortly, gripping Vivian by the elbow, a gun in his hand.

Shark put on a mildly surprised face.

"I thought you'd have more of your goons with you," Fowler laughed when he saw Shark's face. "Maybe I didn't need my little insurance policy after all."

"The merchandise is in there." Shark jerked his thumb at the closed door of 178. "Give me the cash and Vivian and it's all yours."

"How about you give me the merchandise and I let her walk out of here."

"Whatever deal you and Big Paulie had," began Shark, and Vivian glared at him as though she couldn't believe he was still trying to go through with the plan, "we can go back to that. Just let Vivian go and we can talk about it."

"Fuck you. The time for negotiating is over. Open the door." Fowler shoved Vivian at the storage unit. She stumbled forward on her ridiculous shoes. Fowler kept Shark covered as Vivian slid the door open. She hesitated as she reached for the light switch.

"There's nothing in here," she said. "It's empty."

"What?" Fowler swung the gun off Shark and toward Vivian as he stepped forward. Vivian slammed the sliding door closed against his arm. The gun went off, its bang amplified by the metal walls and concrete floors. Shark kicked Fowler in the chest, and as Fowler staggered back, he heard Fowler's gun clunk to the floor inside the storage unit.

For a moment, Shark thought Fowler would stand and fight. Instead, he turned and sprinted toward the exit. Shark ran after him, catching him in a tackle. Fowler elbowed him in the skull. Shark kneed the bulkier man in the ribs, following it with a punch to the gut. Somewhere in the scramble he felt the wire tear off and the recording device go crunch. Apparently, the suburbs also couldn't afford shock-resistant hardware.

With a roar, Fowler pushed off the floor, punching. Shark twisted, blocking what he could. He kicked out, landing a solid blow against Fowler's leg, then followed it with punches to the face and body. He felt a sharp crunch as one of his punches landed on Fowler's nose. Fowler reeled back and fell against the wall, wiping blood out of his face.

"I know you and Flood are in this together," he said, spitting out blood. "I know you got some sort of scam going. I know she's covering your ass for Big Paulie. I don't know how you got out of the Abernathy charge, but it had to be her. I asked around, you're the only case on her docket. Those fucking shoes? She's not a PO. What is she, FBI? Homeland Security? I can be useful to you. I know where all the bodies are buried. Bring me in to whatever scam you're running. We could make this work."

Behind him, he could hear Vivian's shoes clicking down

the hallway and he turned to look. As he turned, Fowler ducked down, reaching for his ankle. Not waiting for him to pull out the drop piece, Shark kneed Fowler in the face.

Fowler collapsed back onto the floor. Vivian smiled warmly at Shark as she stepped up to Fowler's unconscious body, carrying his gun and wearing a pair of gloves.

"He was shooting at me," she told Shark, taking the small .38 out of Fowler's ankle holster. She fired it down the hallway, then tucked it into Fowler's hand, forced his index finger against the trigger. The gun went off again, the bullet burying itself in a nearby wall. Gun powder residue accomplished, she gave the first gun to Shark.

"You acted to defend me. You shot him with the gun that you wrestled away from him."

Her hand firmly on his, she pointed the gun at Fowler. "Pull the trigger," she ordered. "If he knows about Big Paulie or some other dirt then he's a threat to me. I'm not going down because you can't hide your bodies. This makes you a hero. Pull the trigger."

Shark didn't have to ask about the consequences of disobeying. He did as he was told. There was the muffled thump of the bullet hitting meat and he knew Fowler wouldn't be opening his mouth ever again.

The cops came in moments later. Everything went exactly as Vivian had said it would.

Saturday ~ December 31

Shark: The End

"This is inconvenient," Geier said, striding into the open area of the Warehouse. He was wearing a tuxedo, diamond cufflinks, and a watch that a rapper would have been proud to own. His hair, as usual, was a silvered masterpiece of styling product. "We couldn't just meet at the restaurant?" He looked Shark over. "You've looked better." Crease came in behind him, also wearing a tuxedo. Not quite the same level of dashing though.

"Sorry, but I spent all night with the police." Shark didn't get up from the lone dark brown chair in the middle of the floor. "There was a bit of a thing."

"You're not going back to jail, are you?" demanded Geier, looking peeved.

"No. Actually, it turns out I might get some sort of citizen's medal. We'll see."

Geier raised an eyebrow. "Sounds unlikely."

"Yeah, but we'll see what happens after my lawyer gets done yelling at them. Meanwhile, I thought you should know that I solved the problem with the ATF agent."

"Good. I expected you to. Is that all?"

"Not quite," Shark glanced over his shoulder at Marko, who snapped his fingers. Eddie and Beef came forward, each carrying a box. "I also solved your other problem."

Geier eyed the boxes without opening them. "What other problem?" He hadn't reached his age with a full complement of fingers by rushing to open boxes. He snapped his fingers at Crease. Reluctantly, Crease came forward and tore the tape off the first box.

Shark waited until Crease flipped open the lid to reveal the stacks of baggies all marked with a single red diamond. "The supply line problem. My ATF agent has been selling confiscated drugs and weapons to the Scarecrow Jack mob."

"He's dead?" Geier asked through clenched teeth, his face a study of rage.

"Yes, but you may want to send Crease to have a little chat with your friend Fardisburger in evidence lock-up. I have emails saying that he was the source of the merchandise." Shark stood up and straightened his coat. "Anyway, I didn't think you'd want those dropped at the restaurant."

"No," said Geier. "No I wouldn't."

Shark gestured to his crew and turned to leave.

"Shark, when did I say I'd get you back in the city—April? Let's think about maybe making that February or March."

Shark shrugged. "You're the boss." He waited until they were out of the building to smile.

After he dropped Marko and the guys off, he headed for his condo. He smelled like he'd been too close to Vivian, combined with the oily smell of the U-Store It floor. He wanted a shower and a nap in the worst way. He had just reached home when a text pinged through from Peri.

Silly question—but pineapples or cherries?

He was about to reply when he decided he'd wait to get inside and ask for comparison photos. He bounced up the stairs. One of the neighbors was blasting Motown, and he added a Temptations spin at the top of the stairs. He laughed at himself as he felt his cracked ribs protest. Best day ever. Bad guys down. Bank account up. Best girl to see later. Who cared about ribs? Vivian was a problem, but when was she not a problem? She could wait.

He put his key in the lock and stopped. The door was already unlocked.

He withdrew his key and considered his options. Putting his keys away, he pulled out his pistol and slithered through the door.

Peri's uncle was waiting for him in the living room. All of Shark's hidden drop pieces were resting on the coffee table. Al was holding his own pistol, a basic model Sig Sauer, resting it on the arm of the chair, easily covering Shark's approach.

"Hi, Shark. We never officially introduced ourselves. I'm Al Hays."

Shark considered his options. He felt totally unprepared to deal with parent types. He knew how to treat those who pulled guns on him, but Peri would probably be pretty miffed if he killed her uncle. He holstered his gun.

"So glad you could drop by," he said sarcastically, wondering how much time it would take him to put everything back.

"I thought we should talk," said Al.

"Sure, let's talk. But I need a beer. Do you want one?"

"I already got the piece out of the freezer," Al called after him as he walked to the kitchen.

"Yup, saw that. Do you want a beer or not?"

"I'm on the wagon," said Al.

"Suit yourself. What did you want to talk about?" As if he didn't know. He sat across from Al and twisted the cap off his beer.

"Let's talk about my problem."

"What's your problem?"

"Last night I came home to find my niece covered in blood and when I asked her about it, she got annoyed."

"That is a problem. She gets violent when annoyed."

"My niece is seventeen," said Al. "And she likes to solve the little issues at her high school. Which is fine. If she wants to be the biggest badass on campus, then sure, why not? But this," Al gestured to the table full of weaponry, then pointed at Shark, "you, are not high school."

"Pretty sure I'm at least junior college." Shark debated correcting Al's misapprehensions about Peri's level of skill, talent, and amount of shit she was neck-deep in. But that wasn't his place.

"You're going to end it," said Al.

"Relax. She just ran a few errands for me. There's nothing to end."

Al tossed a photo onto the coffee table. With reluctance Shark picked it up. It was a picture of a snowy sidewalk—he thought they were outside the coffee shop. He had his arm around Peri and she was laughing up at him. He knew that no amount of lying was going to make Al believe that there was nothing between them. "We look really happy," Shark said.

"Yeah, you did. And now that's over."

"Or what?" asked Shark. He didn't scare that easily. Peri was worth fighting for. "You're going to shoot me? I'm not questioning your willingness. I'm just saying between my parole officer and my associates, that may not be the smartest plan."

Al chuckled mirthlessly. "How about this? Stop seeing her, or I tell Peri what a bad human being you are."

Shark cracked a grin. "Wrong threat."

Al tossed another photo onto the table. Shark didn't have to pick it up to see that it was a picture of Vivian, dressed in her panties and his shirt, standing in front of him on the balcony, her arms around him. Unlike the other picture, he didn't look particularly happy.

"End it or I will. One of those two won't be happy to see these pictures."

How long would it take Vivian to track down Peri and figure out how old she was? To figure out she'd been involved in Fowler's setup? Would she arrest Peri or just send Shark back to prison? Or worse yet, would she use Peri the way she was using him?

Shark took out his phone. Can't make it tonight. Have to stay in the city.

He tossed the phone over to Al, who checked it and dropped

the phone on the table. Then he stood up, holstered his gun, and walked out of the apartment.

Shark finished the beer in one long swallow and turned on the gas fireplace. He dropped the photo of Vivian into the flames first, but it was a long time before he let the other one go.

Peregrine: The Beginning

"Good you're here," said Al, as Peri unlocked the door. He was staring at the pile of takeout menus she kept clipped to a magnet on the fridge. "What's that thing I like that you order?"

"Pizza?" She really didn't want to be here.

"Ha. Ha. I meant from the sandwich place."

But it wasn't like she had anywhere else to be. Her other option was eating ice cream alone in bed and watching other people have fun on TV. Which sucked because she'd been intending to have more fun in bed—ice cream optional—with Shark. She couldn't understand why Shark had blown her off. He'd seemed so certain.

"Bacon Chicken Ranch," she said tiredly.

"Great. What do you want?" Al was far too cheerful for her current mood.

If it had just been a missed date, then her pride would have smarted, yes, but this had been more important than *just* a date. It wasn't just her ego that was bruised. Her heart was stung. "I don't care."

"Don't you order the weird salsa thing?"

"Sure, that's fine."

Watching her, he called the restaurant. She ignored him. After their argument yesterday about the bloody clothes on the bathroom floor, she hadn't expected him to talk to her for at least a week. Apparently, the rules really were different with sober Al.

She sat at the kitchen table and stared at the map he had laid out. The morning paper had been dropped on top of it.

ATF AGENT KILLED IN STING.

She'd already read the article. It blew a lot of hot air up the skirt of the local PD—Agent Fowler had been selling guns out of ATF evidence lock-up and smart detective work had le to a sting operation. No other crimes were discussed. Shark and his parole officer only got one mention and that was below the fold.

"Are you sure you don't have any plans?" Al asked, hanging up. "It's New Year's Eve. I figured the drill team would be whooping it up or something."

"No, no plans."

"I see your friend Fowler got himself a one way ticket to the morgue."

"Yeah, the cops got something right for once," said Peri. "I told you I wasn't going after him."

"Yeah, the cops," said Al. "Too bad they didn't turn up anything that linked him to sex trafficking."

"I told you it was just a feeling," said Peri, moving the newspaper and staring at the map. "I guess I was wrong." It wasn't the only thing she'd gotten wrong this time around. She just didn't understand how she'd been that wrong about Shark.

The map had a red dot in the middle and lots of little X's that formed a circle around that.

"What am I looking at?" she asked to change the subject.

"The red dot," Al, said, sitting across from her, "is Happy

Place Youth Center. The X's are locations kids have gone missing from."

Peri looked at the broad empty circle around the facility. "None of them are within five miles of Happy Place."

"That is correct. Exactly five miles in several cases."

"That seems statistically…improbable," Peri said.

"Try impossible. Purely based on statistics, there ought to be some within the five-mile radius. Do you know what this means?"

Peri stared at the red spot on the map. "It means we finally have a place to start."

SHARK'S HUNT

Twenty-something Shark Santoyo knows his life is complicated. He's a top level lieutenant to Geier, head of The Organization, he's now working with the FBI, and he's in love with Peregrine Hays, the girl who saved his life with her sharp knives and even sharper mind. Blackmailed into abandoning Peri, by her uncle Al, the ex-special forces private investigator, Shark focuses on his mission—getting out of The Organization. But it's a mission complicated by a brewing gang war and a vindictive FBI agent. With the danger mounting, Shark may be forced to rely on Al to not just make it out alive, but to save Peri.

Shark's Hunt Sneak Peek...

One Week Ago

Peregrine: The Ditch

"You sure about this, Peri?" asked Otto, looking around at the trees.

Seventeen-year-old Peregrine Hays checked her phone again. Outside the car, rain slapped at the windshield, battling the wipers and obscuring the line of trees along the road. She knew that Otto, her Ukrainian immigrant Lyft driver and occasional chauffer, disliked trees and wildlife—he was always happier closer to concrete—but she couldn't quell her own nerves until she saw Tara. The app she'd put on the other girl's phone pinged her location as only a little distance away. She just needed Otto to hang in a little further.

"Slow down. She should be just up ahead. It doesn't look like she's moving," said Peri.

Otto did as he was told.

"There," he said pointing through the windshield wipers as they squeaked across the glass. Tara's car was parked on the side of the road, tail lights glimmering red in the early dusk.

"Pull up behind her," said Peri, pulling on the super tight, trendy leather-look gloves she'd picked up recently. There were more holes to the gloves than glove, but warmth wasn't really the point. Not leaving finger prints was the point. "Keep the engine running." She unclicked her seat belt and pulled out one of her knives, flicking it open as she exited the car.

She stood for a moment, watching the car for movement and telling herself that everything was going to be fine. Peri wasn't thirteen anymore. Things were going to be different this time. Tara wasn't going to end up like Vicki.

Taking a deep breath, she approached the passenger side, peering through the windows, looking for Tara. The car wasn't running, and the lights were starting to dim. The battery was dying. The driver's door was open. She went around to the driver's side. There was blood on the seat and on the grass beside the car—it looked black in the white light of Otto's headlights. She followed the trail down into the ditch by the side of the road.

The ground around her was soaked with blood. Tara's eyes were wide-open and staring at the rain drops as they hit her. Her blonde hair was in limp clumps. The bullet hole in her stomach was a dark flower on her shirt.

Peri reached out to touch Tara, seeing the echo of her thirteen-year-old hand stretching out to touch ragged hole in Vicki's chest. It had seemed then like the hole was larger than Vicki, but the damage to Tara's body was discretely hidden by her clothing. They were different, but somehow still the same.

Just as when she had been thirteen, she knew she should feel more upset. At the time, she had assumed that whatever drug they had given her was blocking her emotions because instead of feeling sad or afraid all she felt was a cold churning anger. As she touched Tara, Peri could almost hear the clank of the handcuff around her wrist. She could almost see blood spatter running up her arm.

Peri knew that Tara wasn't Vicki.

Vicki had been Peri's best friend since they were five. Vicki had been the one who helped her limp home after the disastrous bike crash on Tillman's Hill. Vicki had been the one to help her work up the courage to give RJ a Valentine in fourth grade. Vicki was the first person she called to tell about anything. A hundred sleepless sleepover nights full of giggling. Endless summer afternoons in the backyard. Winter snow angels and throwing snowballs at boys and running.

Tara wasn't Vicki. But Tara had been someone's Vicki.

Now someone had taken all of that away.

Just like someone had taken Vicki away.

"*Vybliadok!*" Otto was standing behind her with an umbrella and staring at what was left of Tara.

"Go back to the car, Otto," said Peri, standing up and putting her knife away. She'd tried it her uncle's way. She'd tried staying in the background—uninvolved and safe—and now Tara was dead.

Otto didn't move. She felt impatient at his paralysis. They didn't have time for the emotions that Tara deserved. She brushed past him and went back to Tara's car, picked up the phone in the cupholder. It had 911 already dialed, but the call had never been sent. She flipped through the apps and deleted the one that linked their phones and dropped the phone back into place.

"Get back in the car, Otto," she said.

"We shouldn't leave her here," argued Otto. "It's not right."

"No, it's not." Just like it hadn't been right to leave Vicki in that house.

"We should call the police. Someone should pay for this!"

"Someone will," said Peri.

"No," said Otto. "No, I'm not—" Peri turned around and looked at him. Otto backed up a step and shifted his grip on the umbrella nervously. He opened and shut his mouth twice, but nothing came out. "OK," he said, finally.

"Good. Now, get back in the car."

Someone was going to pay for this. Just like someone had paid for Vicki.

Read more in...

SHARK'S HUNT

ABOUT THE AUTHOR

Bethany Maines, a native of Tacoma WA, is the author of action adventure and fantasy tales that focus on women who know when to apply lipstick and when to apply a foot to someone's hind end. When she's not traveling to exotic lands, or kicking some serious butt with her black belt in karate, she can be found chasing after her daughter, or glued to the computer working on her next novel.

OTHER WORKS BY BETHANY MAINES

CARRIE MAE MYSTERIES
Bulletproof Mascara
Compact With The Devil
High-Caliber Concealer
Glossed Cause

SAN JUAN ISLANDS MYSTERIES
An Unseen Current
Against the Undertow
An Unfamiliar Sea

SHARK SANTOYO CRIME SERIES
Shark's Instinct
Shark's Bite
Shark's Hunt
Shark's Fin
Peregrine's Flight
Shark's Blood

THE DEVERAUX LEGACY
The Second Shot
The Cinderella Secret
The Hardest Hit
The Fallen Man

THE SUPERNATURALS
Wild Waters
A Little Red
A Deeper Blue
A Brighter Yellow
Maverick
Hudson
Killian
Alekos

GALACTIC DREAMS
When Stars Take Flight *Vol. 1*
The Seventh Swan *Vol. 2*
A Book Excellence Award Winner
The Beast of Arsu *Vol. 3*

Find out more at:
BethanyMaines.com

www.ingramcontent.com/pod-product-compliance
Lightning Source LLC
Chambersburg PA
CBHW070056260626
47160CB00004B/1223